BLOOD OF A HUNTSMAN

After Darkness Falls Book Two

MAY SAGE

Blood of a Huntsman
(After Darkness Falls #2)
May Sage
Cover by Clarissa Yeo of Yocla Designs
Photography by Lindee Robinson
Edited by Cara Quinlan
Proofread by Theresa Schultz

Slayer Blades

CHAPTER

1

C at remembered the first time she'd held a sword. It had been heavy and awkward in her chubby little hands. She'd cut herself that day, and the day after. A kinder tutor might have given her a light wooden practice blade more suited for a five-year-old. Instead, she wielded a jeweled, curved blade with a silver handle that a woman twenty years older might have found awkward.

Kindness had no place in Stormhall, home of her forefathers, some of whom still roamed the marble corridors.

Twenty-three years after that lesson, her grip was light and effortless on any sword, but this one felt particularly nice. Well-balanced. She circled her wrist and marveled at the perfect, fast swing.

"You like it?"

She reluctantly lifted her gaze from the blade to her host, a dark-haired, dark-eyed ancient as handsome as he was powerful. And terrifying. Leviathan De Villier could destroy her on a whim if he so desired.

And when she'd first arrived in Oldcrest, his territory, she'd believed he just might.

She'd been able to tell from the start: he disliked her. No wonder. Catherine Stormhale didn't possess many likable qualities, and didn't care. She wasn't here to win any popularity contests. Cat was in Scotland because, regardless of Levi's opinion of her, this place was a definite improvement over where she came from.

He seemed a little less intimidating these days. Not friendlier, exactly, but when she looked into his eyes, she no longer saw mistrust or hostility. Just indifference, a change she knew was due to his partner. Girlfriend. Mate. Cat didn't know what to call Chloe Eirikrson. They were downplaying their relationship, living separately, dating like they were mere mortals.

"It's beautifully crafted. I can't believe it feels so light, despite the size," Cat told Levi, her blade hitting the air as she lunged to test it further.

She was in his armory, waiting for Chloe. They'd arranged to meet here at seven in the evening. Chloe was late, but Cat knew not to take it to heart. She and Levi had been "otherwise engaged" upstairs—Cat would have known that even if her hearing weren't so acute.

"The trick is ensuring the grip is the same weight as the blade to keep it balanced. Not an easy feat with a longsword. But I had it made in Castile. They knew their trade, back in the day."

Shit. The kingdom of Castile had been dissolved almost a thousand years ago. She definitely shouldn't have just helped herself to a treasure such as this. But the sword hadn't looked that old. A preserving spell, no doubt. Levi had access to many witches, of course he would have ensured that his possessions endured throughout the ages.

Cat put the sword back down on its display. "Sorry, I should have asked before touching it."

Levi allowed himself a half smile that wasn't kind or pleasant; she felt like he was mocking her, somehow.

"Polite as always," he noted. "Don't fret. It's nothing special. A dozen such swords exist. I used to arm my slayers with them. Only three of them are alive now, so the nine spare swords are gathering dust."

"Three of your slayers are a thousand years old?"

Cat shouldn't have been surprised.

A little over two thousand years ago, the goddess Ariadne created their kind, turning seven humans into the first vampires. Those seven humans had, in turn, bitten and turned many mortals. But unlike the turned vampires, the founders were able to reproduce, give birth to creatures made to become immortals.

Cat and Levi were born vampires, though they weren't in the same league. Ariadne had turned Arthur Davell, Levi's father. In contrast, Cat's mother, grandfather, and great-grandfather had all been born into this life, descending straight from the matriarch and founder of her family. She was a watered-down version of Levi.

That wasn't quite fair. Power didn't automatically fade with each generation. Cat's brother Seth was proof of that. But *she* didn't hold a candle to Levi, and she knew it.

The founding seven had often been at war—with each other, with witches, with other immortals. Sometime around the ninth century, they started turning and training gifted humans to send them to battle as foot soldiers: their slayers.

The Stormhales had a few, and it was rare for them to survive decades, let alone hundreds of years.

"Yes," the ancient confirmed.

"I've never heard of slayers who lived to that age," she admitted.

"I believe in taking care of my people."

His *people*, he'd said. Not his subjects.

Her family saw anyone who wasn't a Stormhale as other, *lesser*. Disposable.

Levi didn't. Cat couldn't decide whether he was noble, or playing some kind of game. To appear less threatening, perhaps. If so, it wasn't working.

"Mikar," Cat guessed, naming Chloe's bodyguard. She knew he was one of the men Levi trusted above all. Though it was hard to tell the age of a man permanently frozen in his prime from his aura, Cat guessed that he'd been turned into a vampire a long time ago. "He's one of your ancient slayers."

He inclined his head in acquiescence. "Yes. The other survivors are Sylvan, who's working in the Americas for me, and Ruby. She's around here somewhere."

Cat shivered. Oh, she knew Ruby was around. All vampires knew about Ruby. She hadn't realized that the disturbing vampire was one of Levi's slayers, but it made sense.

The majority of immortals learned to adapt with time. They wore modern clothes, used technology, embraced plumbing. Then there was Ruby.

She wore a white chiton, generally covered in dirt and blood, and wandered Oldcrest at night, running so fast that humans rarely even saw her. Her eyes were wild, her hair tangled and messy. She was responsible for all of Oldcrest's ghost stories.

Cat had asked around about her in her first week.

"That's probably Ruby," Blair had told her. "She's harmless as long as you leave her alone. More or less. I mean, she's paranoid and crazy, but stay out of her caves and she won't bother you."

Cat had frowned. "But what does she eat?"

"Anything, really. She likes to fish. And she hunts game in the Wolvswoods, too, draining them first, then cooking the meat. Waste not, want not."

The heathen wandered Oldcrest as she pleased, draining and barbecuing animals to feed herself, and everyone was fine with it.

"They still have their swords," Levi continued, "though I doubt either use them much these days. They aren't what one would call fashionable."

Cat rolled her eyes. "A good blade is a good blade. Never mind about fashion."

Levi looked at her feet, clad in red peep toe pumps, and wordlessly lifted a brow.

She laughed. "Shoes are different."

"Women. Glad to see the ages have not changed your sex." He walked to the display case and retrieved the sword she'd just put down. "This one is Lightning. It belonged to Rayna, one of the most bloodthirsty females I've had the pleasure of training. She was an artist with her blade. I lost her to the feral curse before we knew about the cure."

There was but one illness affecting vampire kind, a blood sickness. Once infected, vampires became mindless beasts with no desire other than their next meal.

They could be controlled, to an extent, by witches, curses, and binding spells. But by that point, they were things. Senseless things. For thousands of years, there had been no hope for anyone bitten by a feral. Now, they knew of one cure: the blood of Eirikr, the first vampire ever turned by the goddess who created their kind.

And the blood of his descendants. Right now, that meant Chloe and her elusive brother, Tom.

"Lightning," Cat repeated, her eyes zeroing in on a small bolt etched at the base of the blade. The name suited the sword.

"Yes. I thought it appropriate."

He handed her the sword, hilt up.

"It's yours."

Cat narrowed her eyes, mistrustful of any gift freely given by one of their kind. Particularly one as old as the Leviathan. There was always a price.

Before she could say anything, she heard footsteps thumping down the staircase at high speed and then approaching the armory; a moment later, a freshly showered Chloe appeared.

Sweat and Blood

CHAPTER
2

C hloe's hair seemed darker at the roots when wet, but, as always, it grew silver after an inch. Her eyes were currently brown, but Cat had seen them turn bright blue dozens of times— when Chloe was hungry, thirsty, concentrating, thinking too hard, or not thinking at all. The eyes of any vampire could change when they were using their power. But with Chloe, the change was so very natural, casual. She didn't even realize that everything about her embodied power.

Cat's eyes hardly ever changed. She was nothing like the newly turned immortal.

A little white cat with bright orange pupils purred in Chloe's arms. An adorable little monster who didn't accept scratches from anyone but Chloe and Levi.

"Hey, Catherine!" Chloe said cheerfully, before cooing, "Ooooh! Fancy. Is that the sword?"

Cat looked from Levi to Chloe.

"Yes. I believe Catherine was about to decline it,

however. No doubt she shares your belief that presents are somewhat cursed."

Chloe groaned. "You gave me a thousand-dollar coat before we even knew each other's birthday, my immortal idiot. That's not okay." Then, she looked up to Cat, pouting. "Come on, you must take it. I thought so hard about how I could thank you for all the lessons. This is the least we can do."

The present came from Chloe? That was a very different matter.

Chloe was also a vampire, and Cat refused to believe that she didn't have a motive, scheme, or reason behind her actions. But while Cat feared Levi, like anyone in their right mind should, she had grown to view Chloe as a friend.

A novelty. Just six months ago, Levi had accused her of being friendless, and he'd been right.

She had two siblings that she loved, and one of them, she also trusted. She had family, a clan, allies.

And now, she also had...friends. Or something close to it. She couldn't quite trust them, but they spent time together in peace and harmony for no other reason than to enjoy each other's company. When she was with them, Cat didn't feel the need to put up a front.

Well, much of a front. Their world was too merciless to mindlessly bare her throat to anyone.

It was strange. Not unpleasant, but unsettling nonetheless.

"I don't mind training you," Cat told Chloe. "And if you want to thank me? Fine. You can buy me dinner. An ancient sword? That's too much."

Chloe pouted. "You immortals always make a big deal about owing people."

Levi chuckled low and whispered, "Hypocrite."

They heard him quite clearly—vampire senses and all that—but Chloe chose to ignore the insult. "Well," she added, "if you don't let me thank you properly, I'll always owe you a debt for your lessons. That would suck. So, take the sword, please."

Cat glanced at Levi. If Chloe had given her something *she* owned, it would have been different. But this was Levi's property.

"You will not be beholden to me, Stormhale," he said, seeming rather amused. "Trust me when I say that Chloe has paid for the blade *many* times over."

Given the way his eyes shone, Cat could guess how. "Ew."

She grimaced. Neither her friend nor her boyfriend could even remotely be described by the term "ew," but imagining them jumping each other was an unwelcome vision.

Mostly because Cat's vagina hadn't seen any action in a long time.

"All right, then. I'll accept it. Thank you both. Now, I'd better earn that baby. Come on, Eirikrson. Let us see if you still bleed purple."

One of Chloe's most unusual attributes was her blood. The first vampires ever turned, Eirikr and the rest of the seven, had blue blood. The human beings turned into immortals kept the vermillion pigmentation, and Cat, like all vampires born to one of the seven founding families, had black blood running in her veins. No one knew why Chloe's blood wasn't black. Not the witches they'd asked, not the historians, not even Chloe's terrifying ancestor, the mighty and insane Eirikr himself. Chloe had mentioned she'd asked him during one of her visits to his prison.

It didn't matter much. At the end of the day, blood was blood. And Chloe's spilt like anyone else's.

Chloe winced as Cat's new blade sliced her left arm.

"Come on. I showed you how to anticipate that move." By the time Cat was done admonishing her, Chloe's wound had already healed, without so much as a bruise left.

All vampires healed fast, but, as in most other things, Chloe excelled. The newly turned vampire's biggest flaw was that she had zero clue how to use a sword.

Levi had the foresight to show his mate the basics of self-defense before she was turned, so her hand-to-hand fighting was effortless. But Chloe just didn't get swordplay, a weakness she couldn't afford.

Most vampires didn't use guns or other modern weapons; the bullets were too slow, too easy to evade. But in their hand, a sword could move at the speed of light, and they didn't need to waste time reloading a blade. Besides, bullet wounds weren't fatal to their kind. They could only be destroyed for good by a handful of methods. Burning. Beheading. Drowning. Heart completely destroyed, preferably ripped out of the chest. Those were the most common ways to permanently dispose of a vampire.

If Chloe had been anyone else, her inexperience with weapons wouldn't have mattered. But even before she'd turned, she'd been a target. Now, rumors were being spread about her around the world, and thousands of vampires wanted her dead, just because of who she was. What she was. What she represented.

Her line had been destroyed because they were too dangerous, and could—had—risen over their kind in the past. Vampires didn't like to be told what to do, but the Eirikrsons had established laws about their dealings with mortals, witches, and shifters. Those who broke their laws were hunted down and destroyed. Eventually, their kind rose against the Eirikrsons and massacred the entire family. Or so they believed.

One boy survived, courtesy of Levi, and now, fifteen hundred years later, Chloe, his direct descendant, had been turned into one of them.

The entire vampire species feared that she sought to rule them again. The Eirikrsons were the monsters parents told their children about to force them to behave. The vampire boogeymen. It was only natural that their name should incite fear.

Cat knew Chloe. She was just a woman. A twenty-five-year-old, soon to be twenty-six, although she'd stopped aging. She'd worked as a waitress, and until March, her biggest problem had been choosing her thesis subject.

It wasn't fair that the world wanted to kill her just because of her last name. Cat understood this more than most. She, too, had often been defined by her family, her blood. For that reason alone, Cat would help Chloe as much as she could.

As long as she believed it was the right thing to do. And as long as she had a choice in the matter.

"It's a bloody sword, not a cheese knife, woman. Your grip!"

Chloe adjusted her hand around the hilt of her practice sword and tried to lunge again.

Cat moved out of the way at the last moment but admitted, "Better. Much better. Shall we call it a night?"

Chloe sighed in relief. "Please! By all the gods, you're worse than Levi. Are all vampires sadistic with their pupils?"

Cat laughed. Sadistic? If Chloe thought her tutelage was challenging, she wouldn't have survived a day in Stormhall.

At least Cat didn't break her bones when she messed up.

Daughter of Storm

Cat smiled on her way down from Night Hill at ten that evening. She might reprimand Chloe's every mistake and keep a stern brow during their lesson, but that was because pushing the woman was effective. In three months, Chloe had greatly improved; she could no doubt hold her own against most common vampires now.

The slayers, the ancients, and those who owned a house on this hill were another matter. Cat didn't think *she* would have a chance against any of them, so she was ill-suited for teaching Chloe how to fight them. For that, Levi would have to take charge of Chloe's training.

Cat idly wondered if they'd let her sit in on their lessons. She could learn a great deal from the ancient.

If she was still in Oldcrest by then.

She wasn't naïve enough to think that she'd be allowed to remain here indefinitely.

Cat headed to her right, instinctively holding herself a little straighter, stiffer, as she passed a white house built like the Pantheon, with columns, a flat roof, and walls sculpted with symbols from an ancient, bygone world. Everything about this house was familiar, though she'd never entered it. The third house on the hill was but a miniature Stormhall, built to look just like their residence in Rome.

Cat sighed. She'd been foolish to hope that the shadow of her family would not reach her here.

She sped along the path, greeting the keeper of the gates as she left, then rushed down the road leading to the ancient fortress where the Institute of Paranormal Studies had been built.

Long ago, the castle had harbored a witches' coven. Seven families on the hill and dozens of witches in the valley—that had been Oldcrest at the very start. Together, they'd sworn to keep Eirikr locked in his tomb, his prison. For centuries, this hill was seen as the seat of immortal powers, where most of the world's politics were decided in the shadows. Despite her efficient memory, Cat couldn't remember the name of the witch clan, which meant that no one had told her. She filed the question in one corner of her mind, intending to bring it up when she had the opportunity.

Now the witches were long gone and only a few outcasts lived on Night Hill, though members of each family did occasionally pop by.

For Cat, Oldcrest was the perfect hideout. She'd had enough of her family, enough of Rome, enough of suffocating under their rules, their demands, their punishments, but one doesn't simply *leave* the Stormhales. Abandoning the family without orders was grounds for banishment, *if* the head of the family was feeling kind.

Or worse.

More than likely worse, in her case. Aunt Dru rarely felt kindness toward Catherine.

So instead, Cat had been clever, planting seeds and biding her time.

She'd started to correspond with the Beaufort heiress, Anika, a professor at the Institute. She'd mentioned Anika's station, the respect the other families had for her, and, of course, she'd also said a thing or two about Levi being single and highly eligible, until she was finally ordered to go to the Institute. Further her education. Fuck a prince.

Even before meeting him, Cat never had any interest in Levi. She had no interest in anyone who'd want to boss her around. Besides, the stories she'd heard about him were horrific. But it wouldn't do to let anyone think that she didn't intend on seducing him. Cat knew she wouldn't have been sent here otherwise.

Now that it was common knowledge that the Leviathan was with the Eirikrson heir, she expected a letter to come any time, ordering her back home. Each passing week without one was a surprise; she wasn't sure why her aunt hadn't gotten in touch yet, though it didn't bode well. But as long as no word came, Cat would enjoy her freedom.

Hearing a clock chime in the distance, she rushed into the night class moments before Fin Varra, their delectable ancient fae professor, entered the room.

In the middle of winter, Fin often showed up shirt-less—a pleasure like no other on Earth—but now, in mid-May, when everyone else struggled with the heat, he walked in wearing a dark cloak that flowed to the floor like it was made of mist. The creature was unable to look anything but fabulous.

"You think he's wearing anything under that?" the woman seated on Cat's left asked.

Cat grinned, admiring Greer Vespian's courage.

Greer, an ochre-skinned, freckled, redheaded beauty with pale green eyes, was the second woman Cat had ever considered a friend. Perhaps not a close friend—she had no reason to trust her—but they had an easy relationship. Greer never asked personal questions, and never revealed anything about herself. Instead, they joked, gossiped, helped each other in class, and practiced yoga together. Their superficial arrangement was perfect for Cat.

Fin had undoubtedly heard every word; vampires' good hearing was nothing compared to the senses of an Aos Si.

Should the professor not be in the mood to be ogled and objectified, he might spell Greer for months, years, centuries, cursing her entire bloodline with nothing more than a few words.

And Greer just didn't care. Which made her incredibly brave. Or insane.

Cat was wiser; she remained silent, though she did wonder. She couldn't see the hem of any clothing under the cloak.

For a long moment, Fin fixed Greer with a heated gaze.

"I just came out of my bath, Miss Vespian. My skin doesn't tolerate the rough fabric of this world well.

This"—he touched his collar—"came from my world. It's like wearing a cloud of softness."

The witch bit her lip and swallowed a strangled laugh.

"Thank you, sir. That's exactly what women need to hear on these dreary days."

Cat shifted in her seat, feeling rather uncomfortable now that she knew the glorious male was, for all intents and purposes, naked.

"Now, if you're quite satisfied, we can start where we left off last week. It is impossible to spell, hex, or even influence those who carry the blood of the gods, and thus, only one thing can affect them. What is that, Mr. Venari?"

Cat winced and discreetly turned to the back of the room. That was hardly fair.

Sebastian Venari was the newest student in the Advanced Spells class, and Cat suspected he'd picked it only because of the time and attendance. The class ran from ten-thirty to midnight, and mostly consisted of vampires. Greer was the sole student with mortal blood in her veins, and she smelled different than most. Older. Somehow more enticing and less appealing all at once.

To a new vampire, mortals smelled like food. Like prey. Cat had been turned thirteen months ago, and she was still uncomfortable in a room full of regular humans. But strong witches, huntsmen, and shifters were different. A little less like a steak dinner. They had powers of their own, and even the monster buried under a vampire's conscious mind recognized it.

Sebastian—Bash, his friends called him—had just turned, first into a feral, then back into a regular vampire. He was now subjected to the worst kind of desire. A thirst he couldn't control.

And he was dealing with it *badly*.

Asking him any academic questions right now wasn't nice. The guy had bigger concerns.

To her surprise, he grumbled, "Elements."

Correct. Cat's eyebrows hiked up an inch.

Any magic user knew that, but she hadn't expected an ex-hunter to be versed in spells. She wondered whether the huntsmen also had classes on craft. Know thy enemy and all that. Maybe they needed to understand how magic worked so they could kill witches and mages more efficiently.

The huntsmen were part of an ancient, elite order of mortal-ish men and women who hunted rogue vampires, immortals, witches, shifters. Anything paranormal that represented a threat to humanity.

She had little love for them and their tendency to kill first, ask questions later. But for all that, Cat had to admit, she felt sorry for the man. *A little.* No one deserved to be turned against their will. Without preparation.

Until he'd joined the class this week, she'd only seen him a handful of times since it had happened.

And he looked so miserable.

The other part of her didn't feel sorry at all. To be honest, she was pissed at him for wallowing instead of acting. He was such a *waste*.

"Indeed, elements," Fin said. "When you cannot touch the mind or body of your opponent directly, elements are your one defense. Make the ground underneath their feet shake. Make the air blow them ten feet back so they stumble upon their sword.

Command the waters to flood their lungs until they drown."

His voice caressed each word, making torture sound far too enticing. Which was so very typical of a fae, come to think of it. Flooding lungs might be Fin Varra's kink.

"Well, that's the theory," Fin added. "In practice, in the entire history of time, only a handful of magic users have ever learned to master more than one element. Names? Catherine, it's been a while since you showed off."

She immediately named the six recorded multi-elemental mages. Half the class chuckled and the others groaned. She ignored them all.

"Correct, as usual. Now, assuming that you're no Tatiana, Queen of Fae, you will have one affinity. Each individual, even the most mundane of regular humans, has a link to one specific element. This week, we're going to determine your affinity. Some of you already know your power. Very well. Shut up about it and take notes."

Another dig at her. Cat's power was air, and storms in particular; it was in her blood, a trait shared by her entire family. But in this class, she was the only one with a clear familial affinity.

"Elemental magic is as volatile as it is powerful, but control it, and no force in this world can stop you. Let it control you, and it will swallow you whole."

Fin's eyes fell on her, lingering for a moment before he added, "Of course, that's assuming you wield a decent amount of magic to start with."

Ouch.

Shot fired.

Mages and Monsters

CHAPTER 4

Bash didn't know why he'd taken this class. He sucked at this. He sucked at everything, mostly because nothing kept his attention. Nothing but blood.

The ache that had been incessantly pounding at the back of his head for months grew stronger as he followed the professor's instructions and focused on the stone in front of him.

Dammit. How fucking useless.

"You're thinking about this too hard," said a voice he recognized without issue.

His mind—that never stopped these days, even as he slept—only had to hear, smell, or taste something once to know it as well as if he'd known it his whole life.

But this voice in particular rang so very distinct from any other. Probably because Catherine Stormhale, though she was fluent in English, Latin, French, and who knew what else, had the most delightful faint Italian drawl coloring her speech.

He lifted his head and found her looking at him, her pretty face scrunched into a scowl.

She scowled often. Whenever she didn't sneer or roll her eyes.

"I'm no witch," Bash grunted.

"No, you're a vampire," she whispered. "If you had elemental gifts, they would have been awakened when you changed."

"What business is it of yours?" he bit back.

Cat's eyes weren't expressive at all. The opposite. She was so very great at seeming indifferent that he put it down to years of training in the art of being a lady vamp. A predator with a tongue and mind as sharp as her fangs and claws.

But now, he would have sworn she was a little hurt. He refused to feel sorry. He just wasn't her problem.

"None," she replied with a shrug before turning back to her own desk.

He redirected his attention to the blue elemental crystal before him, focusing as hard as he could.

Then, she spoke again, quieter if possible.

"I felt something when you worked on the earth crystal."

Bash glanced at her back. She held herself so damn straight, it was frustrating to watch. Come on, everyone slouched, dammit.

He put the blue stone down and grabbed the brown one beside it.

She was right. Concentrating on that one felt easier, more natural. Although it wasn't doing anything. But at least his head no longer felt like it might split open.

"That's epic! Can you help me too?" Greer, the witch beside Catherine, whispered.

Before she could say a word, their professor answered. "I think not, Miss Vespian. You'll do your own homework. Catherine, that's quite enough flaunting for one day. Behave. If you concerned yourself with your affairs rather than everyone else's, you may have noticed an oddity with your own results."

"I know I respond to water as well as air, sir," she replied. "But that's minimal."

"Does that make it irrelevant, my lady?" he asked her.

Bash could tell Catherine was uncomfortable with this line of questioning, and his instincts were to rush to her defense, do something to help her. That was who he was, and becoming this...thing hadn't changed that, at least.

The professor walked away from Catherine, who relaxed, to Bash's relief.

These days, protecting people wasn't his primary desire. Even now, he smelled everything, everyone. Catherine, Greer, the other students, even Fin Varra. The vamps had told him he'd want human blood. To hunt and drain people. They hadn't said he'd want everyone else's too.

His new instincts cautioned him against the powerful creatures around him. They told him that every person in this room was a fellow predator, not easy prey. But that didn't stop them from smelling delicious.

The very thought made him sick to his stomach.

He was a monster.

His fingers trembling, he dug through the satchel he had to carry everywhere for one of the dozen plastic bags full of blood.

Plain blood that smelled so very boring. Nothing like the scent of actual people.

But it did the trick. At least for a while. After draining the contents of the bag, he could think.

He redirected his attention to the crystal, and, to his surprise, the thing levitated a few inches above his palm.

Quite suddenly, Fin Varra appeared in front of him.

The man made him extremely uncomfortable. He smelled better than anyone else, but Bash knew that even thinking about his blood could be suicide.

"Well done, fledgling. It appears you have more control than anticipated."

Bash had to laugh at that. Yeah, right. Him. In control.

"I just drank blood," he explained. "That must be why it worked."

The professor tilted his head. "And taking what you need negates your accomplishment somehow?"

Bash wondered how often the man complimented anyone. He certainly hadn't heard him do so before. So, he said, "Thanks."

"You are doing well, child. I expect great things of you. Do not disappoint."

Now why did that sound like a threat?

AT MIDNIGHT, BASH MET LUKE AT THE INSTITUTE'S entrance. The brown-skinned, handsome, and slender man who'd been Levi's assistant since sometime around the seventeenth century had been kind enough to volunteer as chaperone when he needed one.

"Ready to go?" the man asked as Bash slid into the passenger seat of his Audi.

He nodded, and without another word, Luke was off.

Just about anyone else would have asked why he hadn't at least brought a change of clothing. Bash was scheduled to spend the weekend with his family.

But he knew he wouldn't. One night, fortnightly, was as much as he could stand. He used to be so close to them, spending all of his spare time with them. Another thing he'd lost, along with his job, when he'd died.

Things could have been worse. He had to keep telling himself that right now so he could manage to appear cheerful when he arrived home.

The drive from Oldcrest to Edinburgh might have taken anyone else around two hours, but Luke did it in one, his fancy, tuned-up car flying down the road. Bash might have said something about the speed had they not both been immortals. The speed limit, like any other law of man, didn't apply to vampires. Besides, his reflexes were considerably faster than any human; they weren't likely to get into an accident.

They parked in a private hangar and flew straight to London in a private jet, treatment Bash wasn't about to get used to. Bloodsuckers, particularly new ones like him, shouldn't be locked in with a bunch of mortals who smelled like snacks for any extended amount of time. But still, they could have just driven there.

Bash tried to consider himself lucky. Actually, he *knew* he was the most fortunate fucker out there. Come on, he'd been bitten by a feral. Normally, that was a one-way ticket to the madhouse, as well as a clear death sentence. The huntsmen would have been forced to kill him. Maybe his friends would have had a hard time doing it, but in the end, they would have done their duty and cut his head clean off. Instead, he'd been saved, brought back to as near a state as possible to what he'd been before the attack. He was himself, mostly. Still liked jazz and blues. Enjoyed reading novels. He could think.

But while his mind had returned to him, the thirst hadn't diminished.

Vampires were the responsibility of those who turned them. As he'd been changed by a long-dead piece of feral filth, he could have been left to his own devices. Instead, Levi and Chloe had taken him under their wing. Levi had power, money, and servants like Luke who facilitated everything he needed. Chloe gave him something even more valuable: friendship. She always had a smile, a joke, wanted to know about his day. It didn't even feel forced.

She'd also offered him a job, of sorts. Chloe had asked if he wanted to be part of her household, an Eirikrson knight. That, he'd refused. He was in no state to be useful to anyone. Or to hold such a prestigious position.

Bash knew why they were so kind: guilt. He'd been hurt when their home had been attacked by vamps who'd wanted to get to Chloe. Somehow, they thought his turning was her fault. Ridiculous. Bash had been a huntsman. Protecting people from danger was his vocation.

Had been.

Now, he was one of the things huntsmen preyed on.

Home

"Sebastian!"

Bash grinned as he entered the foyer of the small but comfortable apartment, some of his fatigue evaporating.

"You know everyone calls me Bash, Emilia," he told his sister, rolling his eyes as he hugged her. Briefly.

Then he took a step back and looked out the window at the seaside to clear his mind.

She smelled...like food.

Shit.

At least the view was a suitable distraction.

His family had lived in Brighton for about four generations now, since they'd been assigned to the United Kingdom.

Ten years ago, at just eighteen, Jack Hunter was moved from the USA head office to England right after Bash's parents were killed. He and Jack had been the same age, but right away, Bash had known who was in charge. The order had sent the English branch their best, youngest agent so that they could keep their shit together after losing their leaders.

Martha and Remy Venari had led the hundred or so English huntsmen until they were killed on a mission. Bash hadn't been given specifics, nor did he ask for them at the time. It was just what happened to huntsmen sometimes. He became head of the family, with a preteen sister and a baby brother. No one expected him to step up and take control of their order here, at his age, while raising kids. He was glad for Jack's presence.

The Venari were given a healthy settlement for their parents' service, along with a pension—Bash didn't need to worry about money, but he still had to help with his siblings' grief, not to mention their homeschooling. The two kids were intent on becoming huntsmen too, and general education didn't cover Vampire Beheading 101, or History of Evil Witchcraft.

He had help. Their people were big on community. Nigh on every huntsman in the country, and some from abroad, came to babysit and tutor, so he managed to keep his own position within the order. But still, he was the guardian of two kids.

Now, Emilia was twenty-one—still a pain in the ass, but she could take care of herself—and Paul had turned seventeen.

They'd be okay. More than okay.

"I'm not everyone," Emilia reminded him, rolling her eyes. "I'm your awesome sister. I get to use your actual name. Come on through. Paul made your favorite."

With a brother who burned rice and a sister only

interested in filleting demon flesh, Paul had naturally grown to become quite the cook. Bash sniffed the air tentatively. Rushes of memories flooded in. Laughter, crying, arguments, jokes. This was home.

Paul had learned to make bouillabaisse from Laurie, a French huntsman who turned up every now and then. It was a time-consuming dish that the teenager only made as a treat, typically for Bash's birthday. That he'd prepare it now showed how much Paul was looking forward to his visit. Bash felt guilty about having to put distance between he and his siblings.

"Jesus, that smells good!" Luke said. "Enough for me?"

Emilia grinned, welcoming as usual. "Always. Go take a seat, guys. I hope the journey wasn't too tiring."

Bash let Luke do the small talk. He was a lot better than him at it. He could lie, remain casual. He could have told his sister that nothing tired him anymore. That he remained wide awake all night, contemplating his hunger for human blood. Wondering whether it'd ever get better. The vampires had told him what to expect; newborns were always thirsty. But he wasn't a run-of-the-mill turned vampire. He'd been made by a sick freak. Some of the insanity, the crippling violent thoughts, were still there, in his blood.

Bash remembered his chat with a young boy named Steven. He'd been cured years ago, but Levi had kept him in his labs for observation, and because he hadn't been sure the feral virus was entirely gone.

Last spring, after running tests on Steven and the rest of the ferals Chloe's blood had cured, Levi had freed them all. They had minders who'd observe them in the upcoming years, but there was no sense in keeping them locked up now that they were better. According to Levi, in any case.

Steven wasn't so sure.

"They don't understand," he'd told Bash. "They think we're like them. But we aren't, are we? It's always going to be there under the surface. The anger. The hunger. The brutality. Your huntsmen friends might have to hunt us down one by one someday."

Bash had said nothing, but he'd felt closer to that little immortal boy than any of the flamboyant people who lived on Night Hill.

He wasn't in control. He may never be.

Bash looked at his family. Emilia was the spitting image of their mother, the same reddish-brown hair and brown eyes, proud nose, and even the mole close to her right eyebrow. His brother was a carbon copy of him. Lighter hair and eyes, broader than most even at his age. They all looked so very similar, but the two younger Venaris were another species now.

"What's with the eyes, bro?" Paul asked.

Bash looked down. He didn't have to ask what had happened. His eyes had flashed in hunger. Not pretty and azure like Chloe's looked when she used her powers or felt thirsty. Crimson. Bright blood-red.

"That's natural," Luke replied for him. "Whenever the immortal part of us is predominant, our eyes brighten. It's a characteristic we've inherited from the gods: Zeus, Hades, Thor, Oden, Kronos. You name one, they get freaky eyes from time to time."

"That's so cool!" Paul was easily excited.

It wasn't that his siblings weren't taking his change seriously. They knew he'd died. They knew he'd lost his purpose, his job, everything. They were just trying to make him feel okay about everything.

Trying, and failing, but Bash still appreciated their effort.

"It'll take a while for Bash to get used to it. But he's improved so much in just a few weeks."

Bash was so very tired of hearing how well he was doing. He knew better than to believe it. He felt like a puppy whose owner praised him every time he went outside to take a shit.

He forced a smile. His siblings didn't need his damn scowling whenever he saw them.

"Hey, I totally did some magic today," he said, knowing Emilia would genuinely flip about that one.

His sister was fascinated with anything that even remotely resembled magic. Always had been.

She didn't disappoint—her eyes widened, her mouth fell open, and she gasped and brought her hands to her mouth.

"You're fucking *kidding*!"

"Just a little magic." Bash shrugged. "I started to take lessons from a fae dude last week, and today he made us work out which element we had an affinity for. At first, nothing worked, but then—"

But then, the unsettling, unfriendly, painfully perfect princess who usually paid zero attention to him had given him pointers. Entirely unexpected of Catherine Stormhale.

He scratched his chin. "Nothing much, but the earth crystal lifted an inch or two."

"I'm so freaking jealous!" Paul cried enthusiastically.

"And interesting," Luke added. "Magic doesn't

come easily to those who aren't born with a pronounced ability. You should be proud. If you can do that at three months old, you might give Levi a run for his money in a few centuries."

Bash snorted. Yeah, right.

Levi was *the* Leviathan, dubbed 'demon of the sea' by those who didn't know better. That whole myth had been born when he'd synced with a massive sea monster and sunk ships full of artifacts that witches had been planning to use against their kind.

Bash was so far from him the comparison wasn't even funny.

"By the way, if you're trying to convince me to not apply to the Institute, you're going about it the wrong way," Emilia said.

Bash's jaw tightened. He wasn't a hypocrite; telling his sister that Oldcrest was too dangerous would earn him a well-deserved kick in the teeth. If it was safe enough for him, she wouldn't hear about it being too dangerous for her. There were evil witches, at least three known major demons, and plenty of vampire dens in Brighton alone, more in London. Cities were infested with evil things, and battling them was their profession. Emilia and Paul weren't safe. They'd never be safe anywhere.

But he'd died in Oldcrest. He'd actually died. The idea of Emilia enrolling in the Institute was chilling.

He hadn't said a thing when she'd first suggested it, but she knew him too well and could accurately interpret his silences.

"If that's what you want," he bit out, slowly.

"But you'd hate it."

"But I'd hate it," he echoed.

Emilia smiled. "Well, Paul hasn't got his first assignment yet anyway. How about we reassess after he starts working?"

Bash tilted his head, frowning. It wasn't like his stubborn sister to relent quite so easily.

"Seriously?"

She laughed. "I may not always show it, brother, but I respect your opinion. Especially when it's valid. The last thing we need is two of us on the front line while Paul is still a minor. Right?"

Now he just felt guilty. She was holding back because of him. Dammit.

"How about you come visit?" Luke suggested. "Bash is staying in Oldcrest through the summer holidays. You could come, get a feel for the place, and spend time with your brother."

Bash was surprised. "Can they do that?"

Luke shrugged. "It can be arranged easily enough if that's what you want."

Yeah. He was a lucky bastard, really. With friends like these having his back, it would be a crime not to get his shit together.

Under the Surface

Paul and Emilia insisted they stay the night, but while Bash usually had a hard time saying no to his siblings, he remained firm on that point. No way was he sleeping in the same apartment as a couple of delicious sacks of blood. He loved them too damn much to risk it, no matter what Luke said about his improvements.

Bash knew what he felt when he sniffed anywhere near them. Pure hunger. In his old life, the only thing comparable had been the smell of bacon after a long sparring session. So fucking irresistible. But even that didn't cover it.

They headed back north in the middle of the night. Another great thing about having a jet on standby.

They rode back through the Scottish Highlands in silence for a time, windows rolled down to enjoy the fresh air.

How sad was it that Bash felt more comfortable

with Luke, a quasi-stranger, than his own brother and sister?

"I'm gonna tell you a story. Not because I want your pity but because you need to hear it. In my days, my people believed in vampires, like everyone does now. There wasn't much proof, and the big, important lords of this world called it common folklore. But my tribe? They knew."

Bash glanced at the ageless creature behind the wheel. He knew the assistant was old. Like, five centuries old, at least. Outside of Oldcrest, he would have been considered a wise, revered elder. But with the likes of Levi on the grounds, it was easy to lose perspective.

"When was that?"

"Sixteenth century, at the start of the slave trade. My mama was taken from a North African country. She was pretty, unluckily for her. I was fathered by her owner. Still, that made me no better than anyone else, just a slave."

If Luke was trying to make Bash feel like an ass for feeling sorry for himself, it was absolutely working.

"Back then, there wasn't artificial blood, see, and vamps fed where they could. Slaves were easier for them. No one really missed us. Maybe some money would exchange hands when one of us disappeared, but if some important landowner had vanished, it would have been another story. Still, people talked in the fields. Even then, there were rumors. We knew about bloodsuckers. We called them angels of death. Angels, because sometimes death could be an appealing prospect."

Bash had no response.

"A rogue came to us in the night. We didn't know what rogues were; to us, all suckers meant death. But looking at him, disheveled and covered in blood, I knew my fate. He went for my sister first—she was pretty, like Mama, see. Pretty is always more appealing, to man or beast. So I pushed her out of the way, and he got me instead. Bit deep. I knew I would be gone in moments. I suspected the rest of my family would be not long after."

Luke fell silent until Bash couldn't bear it. He had to hear the rest. "Well, what then?"

The elder laughed. "Then, another sucker appeared. Different, for sure. Impeccably dressed in ivory. He looked so damn perfect he could have passed for a king. There were more behind him, all bearing weapons. At the time, I remembered thinking it was going to be a banquet, that they'd drain the whole plantation, masters and slaves alike. I'm not sure I disliked that idea. But instead, the sucker pulled the rogue out of me and killed him. One blow and his head was rolling in the field."

Bash could picture it, imagining a mixture of Hollywood movies and any random huntsman raid.

"Levi?" he guessed.

Luke nodded once. "Levi. I was a goner by then. He made a different call, and I rose again."

Bash thought the story was finished. He was wrong.

"And the first thing I can remember is my family running away from us—from me. Screaming. They knew disrupting the masters might mean death, or at least flogging, but they screamed all the way, demanding torches. 'Demon'. 'Monster'. That's what they called us. Me."

Fuck. Bash felt sick to his stomach.

"This age is different. The world has known about us for close to two generations. And your own family, for a lot longer than that. Huntsmen and vampires are at peace. As long as each side behaves, anyway. I get it. New times. But what you have? Do not take it for granted. Do not waste it."

His words held an edge, a subtext that warned if Bash took his family for granted, Luke would make him pay.

Rightfully.

"So yes, they can come this summer. I'll arrange the specifics. Anytime you want to visit them, I'll be there—as long as you believe you can't keep it together around humans, anyway. You got it, boy?"

He nodded, grateful and somewhat ashamed. Two feelings he was growing exceedingly familiar with.

"What's your name?" Bash asked suddenly. "I mean, Luke is pretty modern. Is that an abbreviation, like Levi?"

"The man who fathered me named me something else, yes," he replied. "But I am Luke."

Bash made a mental note to never ask again.

Now that he'd heard of Luke's early days, Bash wondered if he'd been fair to himself. He lived around another newborn: Chloe, who'd been turned the same day as him, and took to vampire life like a fish to water. Of course, he felt like a mess next to her. But, though she hadn't known it, Chloe had been born *for* that life.

He doubted Luke had adapted to vampire life

easily. Bash wondered how many weeks, months, or even years had passed before he'd adjusted to his changes. He opened his mouth to ask when a scent hit his nostrils, so intense and heady he felt like he could faint.

Blood.

So much blood. It hit him like a punch to the guts. Bash growled, a feral, bestial sound no man should have been able to make, as his head snapped east, his mind blank of anything, anyone, save for his next meal.

He crashed into the passenger door, which flew open under his strength, and launched into a run, hunting his prey.

He found them at the invisible border of Oldcrest. People. Students. He knew them, recognized their faces. And it didn't matter. Two were dead, bled dry, their bodies ripped open, limbs torn. One, just wounded, not quite dead, though her cuts were deep and wide. A girl, no older than Emilia.

A sack of blood he was going to drain.

The girl was attempting to crawl to safety. She'd seen something in his eyes.

She could try to get away. She *should* try. He liked a chase.

Bash smiled, and his tongue darted out in anticipation.

His first real meal. This was going to be so much better than the putrid blood bags he'd had to put up with. The beast that crawled at the surface had been unleashed and was entirely in control. The man—the huntsman, brother, guardian, protector—was gone.

Dead.

Then something collided with him. Hard. Something heavy and dangerous.

Bash fell to the ground, but before he'd regained his footing, the creature who'd attacked him had him pinned, one hand around his throat, nails digging into his skin.

He thrashed, growling, and the grasp tightened. Finally, the monster retreated, slowly, reluctantly, as if realizing it'd been beaten.

Now, Bash could see clearly.

The vampire holding him down was a devastatingly beautiful and familiar woman, blonde hair flying in the air. Her eyes were a torrential sky, bright silver, as if made of lightning.

Catherine Stormhale.

"Are you in control?" she asked slowly.

Was he?

After tonight, he'd never think so again.

Bash made no reply.

She let him go anyway.

"Good. We have bigger problems. If you can't handle the blood, get out of here."

Bash didn't think, didn't take the time to look at the blood, and avoided the accusing gaze of the poor victim he'd almost massacred. He just ran, and ran, and ran, until he'd reached Night Hill; then he ran faster, closing the doors of Levi's home, as if to shut the rest of the world away.

He closed his eyes, willing himself to forget what had just happened.

But he couldn't afford to forget.

"Levi!" he screamed, calling the master of the house forward. "We have a problem."

Claw Marks

L evi's famed assistant, the lethal and deadly efficient Luke, arrived seconds after Sebastian dashed through Oldcrest, his eyes narrowed as he followed the vampire's progression up the hill.

Damn, the ex-huntsman was fast.

"Did Bash lose it?" Luke didn't

"I got there in time," Cat replied, stepping close to the surviving girl.

Luke pulled his phone out and started to organize her care; Cat heard him request Alexius, Greer, Levi, all hands on deck.

"It's all right," she said to the girl, as kindly as she could. "I'm not going to hurt you, okay?"

The girl tried to nod but ended up crying instead.

"We were...it was...beast."

Cat wished she could tell the girl she didn't have to say anything, but they needed answers. Students murdered at their borders? The whole world would flip. Oldcrest was one of the safest sup grounds on Earth.

"Didn't see it coming. So fast. It only moved when...the other vampire—"

Ah. So at least Sebastian had done something right tonight, though he wasn't likely to see it that way. The girl would have been killed like her friends had he not interrupted their murderer.

Cat forced a smile. "Hush now. Save your energy, okay?"

The girl hadn't been bitten by anything close to a vampire, or even a feral werewolf. She'd been torn to shreds. Great big claw marks. It was a miracle that no vital organs had been destroyed. Her two friends were in pieces on the grass. Even Cat had issues breathing in this mess. No wonder Bash had flipped.

"I have to carry you," she said. "And it will hurt."

No way to lie about that. They didn't have a choice, though; if they left the girl here, she'd die in the minutes it took to call for aid.

The girl nodded. She was an Institute student. She understood the implications of wounds like these.

Cat was as gentle as possible, cradling her under the thighs and shoulder blades. Then she rushed forward, heading up the hill as fast as she could. Any other time, she would have brought the patient to Levi's home, but Bash would be there. For his good as well as the poor girl's, she stopped at the third house on the hill, knowing that the others would trail the scent and follow.

Six months in Oldcrest, and Cat had managed to avoid entering the Stormhale home. But here she was.

She winced, forcing herself to focus on the matter at hand. Her fingertips pressed on the two bloodiest wounds, pushing them closed as she waited. If she'd had a spare pair of hands, she might have tried a tourniquet, but then again, she had little skill as a healer.

Vampires seldom suffered wounds like these, and they healed a lot faster, so that was a considerable gap in her education.

Cat breathed out in relief when she felt a blast of air, and then a tall, blond, long-haired poser appeared.

"I got it. Well done, Stormhale."

She'd never liked Alexius Helsing. He had a terrible reputation, and everything she'd seen since entering this territory confirmed it. But tonight, she was grateful to him, and also intrigued.

She'd known he was a healer, among other ridiculous things: alchemist, scientist, philosopher. The sort of things vampires didn't care about. But watching his hands expertly examine, cleanse, and sew up the poor girl, she started to admire his way of life.

It wasn't about vampires at all. He'd chosen all these professions to help mortals, she realized.

"I'm here! Sorry I'm late," said Greer, barging in with a big box.

Blair, another PhD student who often hung out with Greer, walked in right behind her, holding a large bag. Cat took the box and bag from the witches and brought them to the healer; given her strength, the weight was nothing.

"Thanks," Greer said, before turning to her mentor. "All right, we brought everything I could think of since you didn't tell me much over the phone. What do you need, Alexius?"

"Anesthesia, first. We'll have to sew up a vein, too."

Greer assisted the vampire. They were a great duo; he barely had to say a word for her to pull out the right flask or instrument. Blair stayed out of the way, handing Greer whatever tool she asked for, holding wounds closed, preparing bandages and threads for stitches. Cat felt like she was watching a surgeon, his intern, and a nurse at work. The only one in the room with no purpose was her.

"Anything I can do?" Cat asked, feeling helpless.

"Fresh water, if you would," Alexius said. "And the girl will need a bed when we're done. I don't want her to move for a day or two."

She was glad to have been given a task.

The house was still in perfect condition; Cat suspected her aunt paid cleaners from Adairford to maintain the premises regularly, even though no one had used it for a whole century.

She'd never been here, but the place was so similar to Stormhall that she had no issue finding bedding, glasses, and everything else she needed.

When she returned to the dining room table, the makeshift operating station, the vamp and witch were both covered in blood and apparently done. The girl was in one piece.

"That was amazing," Cat admitted.

Greer grinned and winked, while Alexius shrugged indifferently. Blair nodded her agreement.

"What did this to her?" Cat asked.

"Yes, pertinent question."

Levi had slipped inside the house without making a sound. Cat was annoyed at herself for not sensing or smelling his presence, but her mind was elsewhere.

On the poor girl, on the unfortunate newborn who'd found her and unknowingly saved her. Above all, on what it meant.

The girl had been attacked by a demon, that much was clear. It could have been a god, but that wasn't their style. The massacre had been too barbaric, too unrefined. Nothing from this world could have left wounds like these and fled fast enough for vampires to lose their tracks.

A demon, here in Oldcrest, testing the borders. That was entirely unheard of, as far as she knew. Demons came in all shapes and sizes, some smarter than others. Like any other sentient creature of this world and the next, they'd been shaped by the gods. But unlike humans, their little entertainment; witches, their descendants; and vampires, an accidental creation, demons had been bred for one specific purpose: to serve them as soldiers.

Most demons, like the gods themselves, were gone from this world. Those who lingered in the shadows knew better than to show their faces anywhere near vampires and huntsmen.

So, what sort of demon was it, and what the hell was it doing here?

She couldn't answer the first question. The second, however...

"These were demon wounds," Greer stated, confirming Cat's suspicions.

She glanced toward her mentor, who nodded.

"Oh, yes. Shadowclaws, perhaps. Maybe something worse. The victim was lucky she got away in one piece."

"Two others weren't that lucky. I just looked at the mess." Levi wrinkled his nose. "It wasn't pretty."

The alchemist sighed. "Demons have no style, no finesse. It's all gore and blood with them."

Cat glared at the insensitive prick. She didn't think it could be possible for him to sound any more cavalier about the whole thing.

"Cat, do you know where Jack's dorm room is?" Levi asked.

She nodded. Jack, like Chloe and Cat, stayed in the right wing, along with the other students who were considered either too dangerous or too powerful to live next door to the rest of the flock. Cat was in control, but as a vampire turned only one year ago, she'd automatically qualified.

She hadn't complained. The right-wing rooms were considerably more spacious, given the fact that only a dozen students lived there.

Everyone knew where everyone was. Jack had taken the attic.

"Good. He can examine the body. Demons are his area of expertise."

Alexius snorted. "Really now? The boy calls himself a huntsman."

"That doesn't change the fact that he's nephilim. He can identify, scent, and track that thing better than us. Cat, get him, if you would."

Cat was surprised. She hadn't realized the man

leading the huntsmen here in the United Kingdom was nephilim.

Scions were the fledglings of gods; young, immortal descendants of the known divinities, such as Lucifer, Zeus, and Chronos. Technically, they could have been called gods, but there was a nuance: scions had been raised here, on Earth, or in the other mortal worlds, away from their prestigious parents. That made them a touch less terrifying than the actual divinities.

The nephilim were half immortal, children born of a scion or god and a mortal person. Cat knew one of them better than most. And she understood that they weren't to be trifled with.

Levi was right. If Jack was one of them, he was the right person to call now.

As she moved to obey, Cat couldn't help but once again notice the difference between Levi and her family. Her parents and aunt ordered her around, no "please" or "if you'd be so kind." A simple "do it" that she was expected to obey without protest or question, even if she didn't understand the hows and whys.

No wondered she liked it here.

But the demon attack marked the beginning of the end. The Stormhales would not let her remain in a dangerous place.

Unless they would somehow profit from it.

Cat wasn't sure what would be worse—going back home, or staying, knowing that she was only here to play a part in their schemes.

In March, right after the attack on Oldcrest, she'd suspected that there were only two options. Either her family would want nothing to do with the conflict or they would be behind it. Each passing day with no letter telling her to pack her things and go home made her feel more uneasy.

She refused to jump to conclusions yet. For now, Cat would just observe and try to understand what was going on.

And when the pieces finally fit together, she would have a decision to make.

Conclave

Bash wanted them all to go, but Chloe, Mikar, and Luke hovered around him, pretending to be "waiting for updates."

He knew that if not for him, they'd be down the hill with the rest of the vampires called to investigate the incident at their borders. They'd be trying to work out what had attacked the three students, doing something useful.

He was just fine. He'd messed up, but no one had been hurt—because of him, anyway. People had warned him it might happen.

Bash refused to let himself crumble. He'd get better. It would get easier. If Luke had gone through this, there was no reason why he wouldn't.

He told himself that over and over. Eventually, it would stick, and start to sound true when he repeated it out loud.

His head snapped up moments before Catherine walked through the doors of Levi's mansion and then headed right to the study, where the small gathering took turns pacing about the room.

"How is she?" Chloe was the first to ask.

"She'll make it."

Thank God.

Bash knew he wasn't responsible for what had happened tonight, but if the girl had died from her wounds, her last memory would have been bleeding out on the ground with him towering over her, smirking like a goddamned monster. He couldn't bear the thought.

She was fine. She'd live, and he could apologize.

Shit. How fucking self-centered was that? Bash had become such a pathetic creature.

"Greer and Alexius were incredible," Catherine added. "She would have been doomed if not for them."

To Bash's surprise, the vamp princess lowered her gaze to his. "And for you, too," she added.

Bash frowned. "Me?"

She almost smiled. Almost. Suddenly, Bash was glad Catherine scowled, because her expression lightening up just a little bit was enough to make his heart miss one beat.

Shit, it was unfair how fucking gorgeous that woman was.

"You startled the demon. Whatever it was, it wasn't in the mood to face a vamp, so it left before ripping her up like it did to her friends. I thought you'd like to know."

He certainly hadn't expected that, nor did he know what to make of it. So, what, his wanting to eat the girl was a good thing, now?

"Thanks," he said nonetheless, because as nonsensical as the notion seemed, he was glad to hear that he'd helped, though it had been entirely involuntary.

"Not just for telling me about her. Thanks for stopping me. If I'd killed her..." Words failed him.

Bash doubted he would have been able to recover from that, no matter what his well-meaning friends said.

"If you'd killed her, it would have been an understandable accident." Luke was firm. "And incidents like that might happen again. You have to come to terms with it."

"Why would he?" Cat questioned.

All eyes turned to her. She shrugged, unapologetic.

"Why would he come to terms with the fact that he failed? Why should he be fine with murdering innocents when it's preventable?"

Catherine wasn't one to speak unless she was obliged to. He didn't think he'd heard her say more than a couple of sentences at any time, in the six months since he'd first seen her. She was all about dismissive glances before getting on with what she was doing. But now that she was talking, her opinion seemed very much in character.

A spoiled, egocentric princess who would accept nothing short of excellence and held everyone else to her standard.

Bash laughed. Chloe and Luke watched him like he'd sprouted a second head, and he realized he probably hadn't laughed in a long time.

"You're a bitch, you know that?" He meant to offend her, but she didn't even bat an eyelash.

"Why, does it sound too much like the truth? I'm not going to baby you and tell you you're fine. You're not. You're a fucking mess. Admit it, then work through it. Simple."

Not one little bit of empathy, sympathy, pity.

And Bash didn't dislike it. Maybe because he'd turned into some kind of masochist. Or just because he was so very tired of being treated like a porcelain doll.

"Anyway, I'm not here to discuss Sebastian's woes, entertaining as they may be. Levi has called a conclave. Everyone will be here within the hour."

Luke cursed under his breath, pulling out his phone as he walked out of the study. Bash heard him give catering instructions to the person on the other end of the phone in a tone that sounded a little too much like panic.

"What's a conclave?" Chloe asked, just when Bash was about to.

"A meeting. Back in the day, it meant a meeting of the seven families on the hill, but since the Eirikrsons were destroyed—"

"Most of them," Chloe piped in cheerfully.

"Well, yes. Since then, there hasn't been much cause for one. Few vampires live on the hill. Levi, Bash—"

"I live in the dorm."

Catherine snorted, like she knew his bedroom was collecting dust. He spent most of his time in this very study.

It wasn't his fault he couldn't sleep. Or didn't trust himself in the dorm, next to other students.

Moments ago, he would have felt just fine telling himself that. But Catherine's earlier remonstrance made him question it.

Sure, it wasn't his fault. But did that mean he was powerless in the matter?

"Anyway, Levi, Bash, Alexius Helsing, and Anika Beaufort are the only residents on the hill. But Levi includes every vampire of Oldcrest in his conclave— me, and the others in the dorm. He's even called the huntsmen to join us this time. It's big."

That explained why Luke was panicking about petit fours. Crisis or not, the De Villier house was known for its flawless reception.

"Right, I think we'd better move to one of the fancy halls, then," Chloe said confidently, leading the way out of the study and behind the grand staircase to a great open space with a high crystal ceiling. The chairs and tables, set up in groups of two or three, were covered with white sheets.

"Give me a hand," she told them, removing the first cover to reveal a dark cayenne loveseat.

Bash started to work on the armchairs across the room while Catherine found a broom and swept the floor. Humans might have taken hours, but speed was the best advantage of their new forms. They had the place sorted in no time.

The red and silver-gray formal hall uncannily resembled just about every throne room Bash had ever seen.

Most of the time, it was easy to think of Levi as a mentor, a friend of sorts. Not in this place. Here, what he was became only too clear.

Royalty.

"Ah. It's certainly been some time since I've entered the hall," Levi said, entering the hall with his hands in his pockets.

Chloe shrugged. "I thought we'd have more space here for your conclave thing."

"Good call, mate," Levi replied. "And glad to see you're making yourself at home."

She snorted. "I'm still not moving in."

"Of course not. That would be far too practical."

The man had a point. When they'd first started dating, Chloe had stayed at the dorm most nights, although she often ended up on the hill right after her classes were over, chilling with Bash in Levi's study. As the weeks passed, she'd started to spend half of her nights here. Now, three months in, Bash didn't think she spent more than a night per week in her dorm room.

Which was better than him. Since he'd moved his stuff from his old room near the rest of the huntsmen to the right wing, where the freaks slept, he hadn't been back at all. Levi didn't seem to mind that he'd claimed his sofa. A chest of drawers where he could keep his clothes had magically appeared, along with a toothbrush for the adjacent bathroom.

"All right," said Luke, stepping in right behind Levi. "The kitchens are bringing refreshments up, and we'll have to open the cellar for wine." He glared at his boss. "You should give me more notice if you want to spare the good stuff. As for the blood, we should have quite enough, but we'll need to place another order of synthetic for—" He cleared his throat. "Our guests."

By that he meant Bash, who was draining their stock.

The older vampire didn't need much blood, a glass every other day; Luke had told Bash that Levi could go an entire week without a drop, quite comfortably. But the newer vampires drank considerably more—perhaps two, three bags a day.

Bash was at ten bags. On good days.

Still, that beat the alternative: taking a bite out of someone.

"Thank you, Luke. Efficient as usual."

"I'll remind you at the end of the year so you can give me a pay raise."

Bash's shoulders stiffened. His attention was pulled away from the easy banter and redirected toward the entrance of the hall.

A minute later, Jack Hunter stepped inside.

Bash's closest friend. Or, at least, he used to be. They hadn't talked in three months. Not once.

Jack abhorred vampires. And unlike everyone else, Bash knew why.

Scent of Blood

*S*even years ago

BASH USUALLY PARTNERED UP WITH BAT ON HIS missions, but tonight, Jack Hunter had asked for him.

Though he was also twenty-one, Jack had already earned all seven stars any huntsman could get, tattooed on his skin with spells and ink. Endurance, courage, knowledge, loyalty, power, empathy, and the elusive one few huntsmen ever achieved: magic.

Bash only had two. Endurance and empathy.

Given his prowess and current position as one of the minds running the London headquarters, Jack could, and usually did, choose to go on solo missions. When he wanted a partner, he usually chose his cousin, Tris—though Jack called her Blade to get on her nerves.

But Jack had requested both Blade and Bash today. For the very first time, he'd asked for extra backup.

Bash didn't need to wonder why. He'd seen the details of Jack's plan; without someone securing an escape route, it was nothing short of a suicide mission. Any other agent would have called a dozen guys for help, but Jack was just that good. Blade would accompany him into the belly of the beast while Bash secured the exit.

A vampire was picking up drunk girls outside of clubs in the middle of the night, and they were never seen again. Jack's preliminary investigation had located him in a den he intended to raid.

Most vampires were loners, scattered anywhere around the world, but some lived in respectable, established clans, like the old families who'd remained in their lands longer than any mortal king.

Other covens were formed much more recently. Out of loneliness, or worse. Power lust. Blood lust. Lust for something else entirely.

These were the vampires who kept the huntsmen busy. Usually, their order hunted down wild shifters gone rogue or black witches sacrificing to increase their strength. They had few dealings with immortals.

Bash considered himself lucky to be picked. He could guess why. While he had learned to use a sword and mace, and could take most huntsmen in a fistfight, his main strength, his best skill, was his eye. He could nail a target fifty yards away with a handgun. Half a mile away with a rifle, in any wind. Against vampires, guns were little use, but arrows dipped in spells and curses could work well enough. For a time.

They wanted him on the roof opposite the

Elephant and Castle den to ensure they were covered when they got out.

And so, he watched them sneak in through a ground floor window, and then he waited, bow at hand, for at least an hour.

Jack came out of the building first, slowly. He didn't look concerned. No one was following, other than Tris.

After observing for a good three minutes and seeing no movement, Bash joined them in the street, jumping down from the four-story townhouse holding on to gutters and balconies.

"Well?" he asked.

Jack didn't answer.

"There were corpses," Blade told him. "Piled up in a room, dumped there, stinking up the whole house. Two dozen, at least. It was fucking disgusting."

Bash gasped. "Who was responsible for that?"

"All of them," said Jack, after a while. "We made them talk. They took turns bringing in women, betting on who could seduce the prettiest one every week. Then they took them, one after the next, spelling them so they couldn't say a word. And after they were done, they drained them too."

Bash had felt sick.

He never asked what had happened to the den, to the twenty-three vampires reported to live there. He never asked about the bites to Blade and Jack, either. Over their dark huntsmen gear, he could only see a couple of bites, but who knew what was hidden beneath the leather and reinforced fabric.

The two young huntsmen had eradicated the entire den.

Before then, Jack had been fair to all races, friendly and diplomatic. But after, there was always an edge to his smile, a shadow behind his gaze when he talked or interacted with vampires.

Two years ago, the man who'd officially taken over for Bash's parents as head of the London headquarters retired. The next logical successor was Jack, who'd led most of their raids for eight years. But some stupid laws said that their leaders had to be professors. Something to do with appearances. As far as humans were concerned, they were a guild of wise, knowledgeable ancients protecting their world. Having a young man representing them was bad. But the High Guard named him leader all the same, demanding only one concession: that he earn a PhD. A suitable title to present to doubtful mortals.

So Jack went to the Institute, and Bash, along with dozens of huntsmen, did what they did best.

They followed their commander.

⚜

PEOPLE WHO DIDN'T KNOW JACK OFTEN THOUGHT that his appointment was nepotism, but the young agent had genuinely earned the British huntsmen's respect. The thought of disappointing him was unbearable. Bash didn't want to see the look in Jack's eyes when he saw him, his best friend, now a bloodthirsty freak.

Seeing what vampires were capable of at their worst wasn't pretty. Bash might not have witnessed it, but he'd seen the horror in Tris's eyes. The hatred in Jack's.

After he'd turned, Bash hadn't been able to face him. Not in his state— mindless, without control, closer to one of the beasts he had to put down in South London than to his old friends.

Tris was a born vampire; her father was a pureblood born from the Drake line, one of the seven vampire families able to bring children into the world, and her mother had been a huntsman—Jack's aunt. Someday, she would turn into an immortal.

Jack didn't hate all vampires on principle. Just the ones who couldn't control themselves. How could Bash face him while feeling like this?

But after three months of avoiding him, Jack was in front of him.

So very tall. So very straight. Jack topped most men by half a head. At five foot eleven, Bash stood taller than some, but he was not Jack Hunter, son of their High Guard and an actual god. A genuine *god*. A minor one, but there was no other word for an immortal born of the old race who'd shaped this world.

Jack was perfect. Bash had always been flawed in comparison, but now they shouldn't even breathe the same air.

He looked down.

Bash heard Jack's feet stomping forward, and half expected the man to punch him. He knew that he hadn't been fair, that he shouldn't have avoided him like he had.

Instead, he encircled Bash's shoulders with his arms and pulled him close, in an uncharacteristic yet firm hug.

"You're a dumb jerk," Jack told him.

But Jack wasn't letting go, and Bash wasn't even trying to get away from the embrace.

Jack had blood in his veins, just like everyone else, and there was a degree of temptation, a part of him that wanted nothing but violence and chaos, that would have desired to sink his teeth inside his neck.

But Bash found that part of him manageable now. Somehow. Maybe because of the three bags of blood he'd downed when he got to Levi's an hour ago, or because of the strange note in Jack's blood that didn't make him feel like prey. The huntsmen behind him also felt stronger. Different.

Bath took a deep breath.

And when he breathed out again, he was still himself.

Voices

C at had sat through many conclaves in her time. All had proceeded in the exact same way: her Aunt Drusilla, leader of the Stormhales, had entered the room, her mere presence demanding silence.

Drusilla talked, telling them of faraway news that colored her perception, her views of the world. She'd give her orders to every branch of the family, naming those who'd failed her in the past for good measure. Then, she'd leave, and everyone else would follow in silence.

The conclave of Night Hill would be nothing like that, Cat realized right away. The setting was somewhat intimate, though the room was impressive, regal. Luke ensured a well-aged bottle of wine was placed at each coffee table.

"Red, white, rosé? Bubbles, no bubbles? Sweet, dry?" Levi's assistant asked, sounding quite panicked.

"If it's wet, I'll drink it."

She had been trained in the art of appreciating

wine, could tell a good one, a common one, and an expensive one, but she'd found that she liked most of them equally.

Chloe, who'd chosen to sit next to her, chuckled. "All right. That was unexpected. I thought you'd be one to roll a glass in your fingers and tell us all about the bouquet."

Cat shrugged. "I can certainly do that when it's required of me."

"What can't you do?" Chloe challenged in a half whisper that carried across the room.

A hall full of supernaturals meant there was no such thing as a private conversation.

The huntsmen may not have senses quite as keen as the vampires, but their ears were acute enough for this distance.

Cat shrugged, conscious of the eyes on her. Of course they were curious. The Stormhales kept to themselves. They didn't mingle, like the other founders. The only people who lived in Stormhall were Stormhales. Even their slayers were rarely admitted to the main house.

"I'm rather average at a great number of things," she stated.

"Average?" Chloe repeated. "Yeah, right."

Cat remained silent, though she could have explained. Her trainers had expected her to be quite good, but she'd never been encouraged to pursue true excellence. Once she mastered a subject, she moved on to the next.

"Languages?"

She asked which one in Russian, to make a point. "*Kotoryy iz?*"

"What did you say?" One of the huntsmen asked.

"Which languages," Mikar, seated next to Chloe, translated for her. "Literature?" the handsome, bronze-skinned elder submitted.

"'Reading furnishes the mind only with materials of knowledge; it is thinking that makes what we read ours.'" Cat quoted Locke.

"Science?" Chloe supplied hopefully.

This time, Cat went for Einstein. "'Any fool can know. The point is to understand.'"

"And you do understand," Chloe guessed, rolling her eyes.

Cat laughed. "The basics. As I said, I was only expected to reach mediocrity. My job isn't to stand out. It's to be of use."

She knew, right away, that she'd said too much. Her friend frowned in concern.

"What do you like?"

Cat turned. Fifteen feet away, around another coffee table, Bash was seated with Jack and a female huntsman she'd seen around Oldcrest. She'd even traveled with her to London, but Cat didn't think the woman had ever introduced herself.

"Pardon me?" she asked, somewhat confused.

"What do you like to do?" Bash repeated. "In your free time. If that's a concept you understand."

Cat stared at him for a good long while. She didn't think she'd paid much attention to him before, in a specific kind of way. She'd glanced. She knew his smell and his presence. She knew he was handsome, well-built, and muscular. But that was about it.

Now she noticed his eyes. Amber. Hair darker, not

quite brown. A tattoo peeked from under the sleeve of his T-shirt.

"Music," she said. "I like to listen to music. And play it. Badly," she added, to be accurate.

"You should play with me someday. I wager you'd improve. I could tutor you in violin, piano, singing—"

Cat glared at Bash.

"For what price?"

Before Alexius spelled out the gross reply she could foresee, Levi clapped his hands, demanding attention, as he stood before a throne-like chair at the very center of the room.

A familiar scene.

"All right. I believe we're all here. Word travels fast, so you know there's been an attack. Myself, Mikar, and Alexius have all examined the bodies, but it's Jack's area of expertise, so let's hear it."

Cat frowned, confused. But Levi had sat back down, letting Jack take the stage.

"Was it a shadowclaw?" Alexius asked.

Jack shook his head. "No, there's no venom in the wound."

"A nightfang, then."

"With your permission, sir, I'll speak now."

Cat's respect for Jack went up a notch; he managed to shut up Alexius Helsing. Not a small feat.

"My huntsmen know the drill—not sure about you guys, so to make it simple: 'demon' is a general term that encompasses too many creatures. Some are made by the gods to fight their battles and guard their homes, yes. But some weren't made at all; they were brought here."

"From the gods' world?" Chloe asked.

Jack nodded.

"Yes. Dragons, selkies, chimera. Whether as pets or just because the gods liked having a living zoo in their transports, those creatures traveled from another realm. The monsters from the old world are considerably more powerful than your average hellhound. I'm by no means a demon expert, but I have one on speed dial. According to my father, the speed of the creature and the marks left on the remains suggest it might have been the work of a greater demon. A manticore, specifically. If he's right, and Rakiel usually is, capturing it will be extremely difficult, and killing it, impossible for us. It's fast, tonight proved as much, but manticores are also extremely clever. There's a reason behind the legends of ingenious sphinxes. Whatever trap we can think of, it will have anticipated it."

"I think," Cat said, as Jack paused in his demonology lesson, "that we should focus less on the manticore itself and more on what it could want here. If it's as clever as you say, why hunt here, with dozens of immortals behind the gate? Unless it likes a challenge, it was probably sent here."

The entire room was listening intently.

Cat wasn't used to being listened to. Especially not in a conclave. Actually, this didn't feel like a conclave at all. More like her weekly naughty book club with her cousins, despite the severity of the situation. Just a discussion between...perhaps not friends, but allies. Equals.

"Good point, but the answer is obvious," Levi said. "As there have been no attacks on our borders for centuries, and in the space of a handful of months, we suffer two, we can only deduce that they're related. Those who got through our gates in March are trying to test the borders now that we've made it harder for them to get in."

"Harder? How so?" Tris asked.

Levi exchanged a glance with his peers, Alexius and Anika. This wasn't a point they'd wanted to discuss here, with so many ears. And her presence was probably the reason why.

Cat understood that. She was a Stormhale. And that made her their enemy. Potentially. Probably.

She shifted uncomfortably.

To her surprise, he answered after a beat.

"We've reworked the way our wards work." Levi smiled. "Well, those we haven't killed. Before March, any resident of Oldcrest could invite someone through the gates. Now, the invitation must come from a current resident of Night Hill. A traitor among us let in those ferals and vampires, and we couldn't afford a repeat of that. The access to our territory of anyone, except Institute students and current residents of Oldcrest, has been revoked. We have a blank state, and security in place to avoid another breach."

Cat stilled. She opened her mouth, but no words would come.

That won't be enough.

That's what she should have said. Now was the time to reveal what she could do, what her entire clan could do.

But it was a family secret. She'd be betraying not only her intimidating, all-powerful aunt but also everyone else. Her little sister and her big brother. All those who relied on secrecy to defend themselves. If the world knew how the Stormhales operated, they'd be prepared for it.

However, if she said nothing, her friends could suffer. Her friends could die.

But only if her family attacked them.

Cat's heart ached. Her brain throbbed. Her throat tightened.

Say it. Keep your mouth shut.

Her mind couldn't settle on an answer. There was no right one.

"Hang on," said a huntsman Cat didn't recognize. "You reworked wards made thousands of years ago? Just like that."

She was grateful for the interruption to her messy train of thoughts. Also, the huntsman made a good point. How the hell had they achieved that feat?

Levi's expression changed, and before he said a word, Cat knew he was done sharing sensitive information.

"Anything is possible with the right tool."

Could his reply have been any vaguer?

"The point is, they can't get in anymore, and they've worked that out. So, they're throwing what they can at us to see what sticks, so to speak. This is the start. They wanted to see if the manticore could pass through once a student opened the gate."

The theory made sense: the creature had hunted its victims down so very close to the border, and the girls had, of course, tried to get back in.

Cruel and insensitive as the feeling was, Cat was glad they hadn't made it across. Because if the manticore had managed to get in, they might have had to bury a hell of a lot more than two bodies.

"Would it have worked?" Chloe asked.

Greer, sitting next to Alexius, nodded. "If it was touching the girl as she passed through, more than likely. But tricks like that can only get one creature in at a time. It's not a viable option if they want to flood our gates with an army again."

"Still, we won't let them pick off our students," Anika stated.

There was a unanimous nod of assent, Cat included. Confused and conflicted as she was, one thing was certain: she didn't want to see other girls torn the same way.

"I propose we reinstate a sentinel patrol, day and night," Levi said. "I will not hire outsiders, not in the current climate. That means that each of you—each of *us*—will need to do our part. For that reason, let's put it to a vote."

By this point, Cat shouldn't have been surprised, but she was. A patrol made sense. Everything they'd said led to that conclusion. Except Levi could have just told them what they were going to do. Ordered them. Not Alexius or Anika, perhaps, and not the huntsmen, either. But twenty-nine vampires were gathered in the room, nine of whom were his employees. He was their lord by every law their race obeyed.

And instead of commanding them, he made them vote.

So that was what freedom tasted like.

No voice spoke against the arrangement, and Cat signed up for the first shift of the day—or the last one of the night, depending on how one looked at it. Half past midnight to six. Most of her lessons ran from afternoon to late evening, and, in any case, she'd never needed much sleep.

Only when she'd written her name down did she notice the first person who'd scribbled his name on that timeline.

Bash.

She looked up, frowning.

Something about him annoyed her. Not because he was a turned vampire—though to the Stormhales, that was a sin in itself. They believed that only the born vamps were worthy of note. Cat had always found that position rather stupid and outdated. There were stronger and weaker vamps in every founding family, the Stormhales included, and the turned were the same. At the end of the day, the blood in their veins might be a different color, but that was the end of their differences.

It wasn't even because he was—had been—a huntsman. His kind had killed hundreds of Stormhales, some without much of a motive.

No, the reason Cat disliked him was because he was a waste. A waste of power. With so much strength at his fingertips, all he did was mope around about being changed.

She got it; he wasn't born like her. He hadn't been prepared. But the change had been months ago. He should have started to adapt, and embraced the fact that he was a greater warrior now than ever before.

Cat remembered when her brother had turned. He'd barely undergone any change. He'd been a powerful mage before, with eyes that already turned as stormy as the night when he called his power.

Becoming a vampire had done very little other than increasing his speed.

Her? Well, she hadn't been much before. Weaker than her little sister in hand-to-hand combat. Not even in the same realm as her brother when it came to magic. She was the typical middle child. Turning last year had also been inconsequential.

But Sebastian...

Cat, like most vampires, had an eidetic memory, which was the only reason she could recall Bash before his change. He'd been unmemorable. Pretty enough to look at, but, given their exercise regimen, most huntsmen were rather delectable. He'd been kind—that, she remembered. When he'd seen Chloe feeling uncomfortable—partially thanks to Cat—Sebastian had intervened. But that was it.

After the change, being in his presence was like standing in front of a bomb ready to explode.

He was faster than her, stronger than her—if he hadn't relented earlier tonight, she would have been in trouble, but the moment she'd snapped him out of his blood haze, he'd stopped fighting.

And he had magic.

Did he even realize how rare it was for a turned vamp to develop actual magic so damn early on?

Cat would have killed to have his strength. And frequently wanted to kill him for not using it.

A Taste of Insanity

CHAPTER

11

The girl woke up at five that afternoon. Jack called right away, and this time, Bash answered.

Her name was Maddy, an undergrad earning her bachelor's in witchcraft.

Maddy described the creature that had attacked her as a thing hiding in gray mist and black shadow, but when it stayed still long enough for her to have a good look, she'd seen a human face with sharp, long fangs, the body of a lion, and a snake's tail.

"I was high, right?" she asked.

Jack smiled tentatively. "I wish. Get some sleep, Maddy. We got this."

Bash hadn't missed the way she looked at him, like he might just be worse than a human-faced, lion-clawed, snake-tailed monster.

He'd stayed as far away from her as possible in her borrowed accommodations within the impressive and cold Stormhale house on the hill.

The girl was still too weak to be moved.

"I'm sorry," he told her. "I just turned and—"

"I know who you are," she replied, cutting him off. "And I know about new vampires. It's cool. The demon left when you came, so it's doubly cool. Seriously. Chill. And you couldn't help yourself. No harm, no foul. Just...stay away from me, please? For now. While I heal."

Fair.

A knife to the chest, but better than what he deserved.

It might make him sound like an ass, but Bash was glad about the sentinel patrol. He definitely wasn't happy that the girl—Maddy—had been hurt, but having something to do, a purpose he was good at, in order to protect people? Yeah, he'd missed that.

After his nighttime astrology class, he headed to Oldcrest's southwest border, near the Wolvswoods, his assigned post.

And he stopped dead.

"Catherine."

What was she doing here?

"Sebastian."

It's Bash. That's what he said to everyone else. What he should have said to her. But somehow, this stuck-up girl using his full name felt right.

"You're patrolling with me," he guessed.

"I'm not thrilled about it either. Never was very fond of babysitting."

He shook his head in disbelief. "Your people skills are horrendous. Didn't they teach you how to be nice, along with all the other shit you learned?"

She shrugged unapologetically.

"Oh, I can be nice. Is that what you want? For me to coddle you like everyone else?"

No. Not at all. Quite the opposite.

Bash was uncomfortable around mortals. Better around huntsmen, Jack in particular. Okay with vampires, because he knew that if he went crazy and attacked them, they could defend themselves.

But he only felt one hundred percent relaxed around one person. Her. Catherine Stormhale. The woman who didn't pity him, and who'd already put him on his ass once. Unlike absolutely everyone else, she didn't smell like dinner, not even a little bit.

She smelled like winter. Cold, crisp pine needles, apples and cinnamon. A delicious perfume that didn't make his throat tighten in thirst.

"You know, I think I'd love to see what you look like when you try to coddle," he replied, amused at the very thought.

That might prove entertaining. She didn't have a shred of sweetness to her.

Catherine rolled her eyes and pointed north of the Wolvswoods.

"All right, you just missed Chloe and Mikar; they said they'll cover the northwest, from this point to the lake on the other side of Night Hill. We have southwest, from here to the border, near the rail. Crysalia and Anika have southeast."

"What about northeast?" Bash asked, frowning.

Catherine shrugged. "Most of that is the lake, and Cosnoc. Levi said we don't need to trouble ourselves with it."

Cosnoc. The hill where Eirikr had been locked up these last fifteen hundred years. Vampires were always tight-lipped about the specifics, especially with hunts-men, but Bash understood that the area was warded, even more than the rest of Oldcrest.

"So no one guards it?"

"No, there are always guards around it. It just doesn't have to be us."

He nodded.

"Should we split up?"

Catherine sighed. "I wish. Mikar was clear—we're supposed to work in pairs. They threw a manticore at the borders, so who knows what it'll be next."

As she wasn't hiding her opinion that working with him wasn't her idea of fun, Bash believed he'd be in for a dull six hours.

He was mistaken.

They were walking side by side, heading south, when she stopped, head snapping left.

Bash halted next to her, frowning, as he couldn't hear anything that would have alerted her.

"What is it?"

She blinked, startled. "Sorry, nothing."

"Obviously not nothing."

She pointed in the distance, through the trees.

Bash knew his sight and hearing had improved after he'd become this thing, but he hadn't had much cause to use either yet. Following the direction she indicated, he squinted, eyes piercing through the darkness.

Then he saw it—a small brown and white owl, picking at her feathers. She was adorable, and Bash couldn't stop staring, looking at each individual feather. He realized he'd never exerted his eyes like this. He shouldn't have been able to see quite that far, and in so much detail. But it wasn't unpleasant at all.

"She's fascinating."

"Animals generally are interesting when left undisturbed. We're far enough away to observe them as they go on with their little lives."

"Do you do that often?" he asked.

She resumed her walk, and he followed, reluctantly turning away from the cute night hunter.

"Not as often as I'd like. There are things to do, lessons, assignments. But I have more time here. I got to you fast last night because I was in the woods when I smelled the blood."

"Watching owls?"

She shook her head. "Drawing ravens. Close enough."

"She draws, too!" He laughed.

"Terribly. I took it up a few days ago; give me a century or two, and perhaps my skills might extend past stick figures."

"Ah! And you didn't see fit to mention that when the others asked what you didn't excel at."

"They were having too much fun guessing to let me say my piece."

Then they fell quiet, as they had a job to do, but after their little chat, the silence was comfortable. They walked down to the southern borders before heading back to the woods. The owl was gone from her tree, no doubt to hunt for dinner.

"Look here," Catherine whispered, eyes on the ground.

He followed her gaze to find a red fox huddled around three little cubs.

The owl had been interesting. The foxes, though...

Bash looked away.

He used to like foxes. Now, they smelled like food. Bland food, but food nonetheless.

Catherine watched him with a frown.

"I'm fine. I'm in control."

She snorted. "Yeah, right. Not even close."

He couldn't protest. It wasn't the foxes, really. But their scent reminded him that he was thirsty. And now he imagined the smell of blood from yesterday. Tons of human blood flowing, seasoning the air. He could almost taste it, making him feel sick. And ravenous. And disgusting.

"You know you're making things worse, right?"

"Look, not all of us are century-old undead, born with a silver spoonful of blood between the fangs."

He'd meant to hurt her, but Catherine didn't so much as flinch.

"I'm a year old, dickhead."

Now he was genuinely surprised. With all her accomplishments, he'd assumed she was as ancient as any of them.

A fucking year old. She was a fledgling, barely more experienced than him.

Sure, unlike him, she'd been prepared from an early age for the change, but Bash wasn't just a regular who was ignorant of the process or what it meant. He'd studied vampires his whole life too.

That shut him up. And made him feel worse.

"And I was never anywhere near as unstable as you. You know why?" Catherine pushed.

"Because you're a Stormhale princess," he snapped.

"Because," she echoed, "I never avoided humans. I

never stayed away, and sniffed the air all the while drinking blood made to imitate theirs, as if to make the temptation even more impossible to resist. You're not letting yourself get used to anything. You're stuck in the first stage, the feral thirst that's meant to last hours, not months."

Bash turned to face her, fists tightening. If she weren't a woman, he would have snapped.

As if the fact that Miss Perfect was a new vampire didn't sting enough, now she was telling him he sucked at this because he wanted to? He'd never asked for this. If it had been up to him, he would have asked for a quick, clean beheading. But he couldn't. Because of his siblings, Jack, the rest of the huntsmen, he had to fight through this. Linger in this world for their sake. Her indifference, her contempt? He didn't mind. But she didn't get to lecture him.

"I think I hate you," he told her, taking one step closer to her. "I've never hated anyone in my entire life. But you? You have everything. Beauty, wealth, friendship. And look at what you do with it. You delight in making others feel small. Shall I crawl at your feet to please you?"

"You're already crawling. If you wanted to please me," she replied, walking forward, closing the distance between them, "you'd grow a spine and stand up."

Then his mouth was on hers, or hers on his; he had no clue who started this messy, hungry, haunting kiss. She leaped in the air and wrapped her long legs around his torso; Bash grabbed her waist and pulled her against him, desperate to feel more, taste more.

Bash had no idea how, or why, since he'd just professed to hate her, quite sincerely. Perhaps because he hated her so very much, he wanted everything. Needed to touch her, sink inside her, make her scream his name.

But right then, she pushed against his chest, unhooked her legs, and jumped back to the ground.

"What the hell?"

He didn't know whether to be confused about the interruption or the fact that they'd been making out in the first place.

"That won't happen again," she said, a clear warning in her voice.

They conducted the rest of the patrol in silence. Bash was confused, annoyed at himself, and pissed at her. Mostly pissed at her.

At six in the morning, they headed to the dorms. She stopped on the second floor and he climbed to his room on the third.

Only when he woke up around midday did he realize three things.

He'd slept. He was in his own room. And he hadn't drunk a drop of blood for twelve hours.

A Residence

Cat didn't sleep. Nor did she deserve to. What the hell? She had no business kissing Sebastian in the woods, no matter how long it'd been since she'd last seen some action.

She'd never been fond of celibacy. In Rome, her family gave her Saturday nights off; she headed straight to hot tourist spots and played with the hottest guy she could find for half a night. Here, there was nothing for miles upon miles, and she'd been ordered not to leave Oldcrest without an escort.

When Levi had asked her to go to London last March, she'd had to call her aunt and request permission.

Yes, it was sad for a twenty-seven-year-old, grown-ass vampire. But that was what it meant to be a Stormhale. If Aunt Drusilla had heard that she'd gone out of the territory after being explicitly ordered not to, there would have been hell to pay. Punishment. Not physical, although Drusilla didn't squirm at slaps when she felt it was necessary. But Cat's true punishments were worse. She'd wait for Catherine to truly fall in love with something, and then rip it away from her.

The first time, it had been her owl, which she'd found wounded outside of their land and nursed back to health. When Cat failed her magic tests, Drusilla crushed it in her grasp. Then, there'd been the piano. Cat loved playing, and at the time, she'd been good.

When she was nineteen, Drusilla told Cat to seduce a visitor. It wasn't the first time that she'd been given such a task, but Cat hadn't fancied the guy. He was a complete tool, and sexist to boot. So she said no, and Drusilla broke her fingers, twisting them one by one.

She remembered that day well.

"That man owns a bank I want to be in business with. And he's not easy to please. But for some reason, he fancies you, a stupid, spoiled brat. So, you will *fuck* Robert for your family, Catherine."

She'd already snapped the index fingers by then.

Catherine steeled her resolve, straightening her spine.

"I won't."

Drusilla moved on to her middle fingers. And then the rest. Catherine managed not to scream or cry, wincing through the ordeal.

She knew Drusilla could have forced her, regardless, but she didn't. And after that day, she never demanded that Cat whore herself again. She'd earned her aunt's reluctant respect.

But she'd lost her ability to play music.

That had happened years before Cat turned, and so the healing had taken some time. Though a competent doctor reset the fingers, she never played again, even after regaining the use of her hands.

The incident had taught her one lesson. She couldn't afford to show what she loved. What she hated. What she felt. Not in the pit of vipers where she'd been raised.

Cat refused to feel.

Hence why that kiss had made no sense whatsoever. She was on a dangerous slope. Because she'd definitely *felt* last night. Lust. Desire. Intrigue.

These were feelings for normal people who had their freedom, not Stormhale heirs.

She sighed, heading out of bed and down to the right wing's common room.

It was empty, as usual. Few residents lived in this part of the house, and they didn't have the same sense of community as the rest of the Institute students. They were the predators. Cat got along with Chloe, but the others gave her a wide berth.

The ground floor was decorated in black and white, like a chessboard, with a checkered floor, black velvet sofas and armchairs, and white tables and sideboards.

Her eyes went to the first object she'd noticed after moving in, tucked in the corner of the room.

A piano.

Six years had passed since she'd played anything at all. No doubt she'd entirely lost the ability by now.

"Hey!"

Chloe surprised her, which meant that her mind really was a mess: vampire or not, the woman definitely wasn't stealthy.

"I didn't think you'd be up already. Didn't you have patrol a few hours ago?"

She nodded. "Yeah. You know, undead and all. We don't need that much sleep."

Chloe laughed. "That's definitely a perk. Fancy sparring, then? I don't have a class until two."

Cat stole one last glance at the piano before turning her heels and heading out of the common room.

"You know what? Sparring sounds great."

❧

AFTER LEAVING CHLOE AS SWEATY AND OUT OF breath as one of their kind could be, some of Cat's frustration had dissipated. She was starting to untangle her thoughts.

Too much had happened all at once. The manticore yesterday, the wounded girl in her family home on the hill, Bash. All small concerns that had effectively hidden why she was feeling uncomfortable. The questions and theories that had robbed her of her peace of mind the last few months.

But now, Cat had an inkling.

The entire situation in Oldcrest felt like a major setup. The term had started in October, so how come she, along with a dozen new students, had turned up at the same time in January? She'd have to check with the administration to be certain, but Cat doubted so many people usually started in the second semester.

Then the demon attack. Why make it so very obvious, leaving bodies out in the open? It felt like a warning more than anything else. Or perhaps a test.

But above all, the most important pawn—set up on the chessboard, by whatever player was carefully manipulating the pieces—was her.

Before March, any resident of Oldcrest could invite someone through the gates. Now, the invitation must come from a current resident of Night Hill.

Cat stayed in the dorm by choice, because she hadn't wanted to lock herself away in a huge empty house. Her current address was Number Three, Night Hill, which meant that she could let anyone she wanted inside the territory.

Her family had let her come to Oldcrest for a reason, and Cat now doubted that it was so she could bag a De Villier prince, as she'd initially thought.

If she was right, her family was against Oldcrest. Against Chloe, Levi, everyone else. Cat knew her aunt too well to doubt that she'd call herself queen given half a chance. They could be the ones behind this whole mess. If Drusilla wasn't the queen, at the very least, there was a considerable chance that they were in league.

Meaning, Cat would soon be given orders she might not like.

As her next lesson wasn't until later that afternoon, Cat walked down the hill at a leisurely pace. She decided to stop and see how the patient was doing, if only to distract herself.

She walked into the guest bedroom, where Greer was changing Maddy's bandages.

"Hey there. You look better."

Ever so slightly. Cat hadn't changed very long ago, so she remembered that it took time to heal from the stupidest little things. Maddy's attack had left wounds as serious as any human could get. Even with Alexius's healing powers and Greer's magic, she wouldn't be walking for weeks.

"Funny. I didn't peg you for a liar." Maddy snorted.

"All right. You look alive. Alive is better."

The girl tried to smile, and gave up after a wince.

"Anything I can get you? Food, a book? Is someone copying your lessons?"

Maddy closed her eyes, as though keeping them open was too much of an effort.

"I'm all good, thank you."

Something changed in the air, all of a sudden. Cat went to the window and looked out at the darkening sky.

Cat went to the girl's bedside table and took her phone. "I'm inputting my number in here. I can't take calls in the Institute, of course, but text if you need anything."

"Everyone offered to help," Maddy replied.

"Well, you're not everyone's guest. You're mine."

She'd learned many lessons she would have liked to scratch from her mind. Hospitality wasn't one of them.

"You're nice. You should let people see that you're nice."

Cat chuckled.

"I'm not even close to nice, Madeleina. But what happened to you was unfair. And what happened to your friends, unacceptable. If there's any way to make things easier for you now, I'll try. As anyone with a soul would."

Maddy's eyes fluttered open. "It's not your soul

that I see. It's your heart. Someday, they'll understand how big it is."

Cat watched the girl closely. She'd asked for her name, but she didn't know much else about her. There had been something in her tone, something that made her words sound like certainty.

"I'm tired now. Are we done, Greer?"

"Just about."

"Good. Can you knock me out?"

The witch laughed and handed her a small flask.

"Sweet dreams."

Maddy downed the contents without question, collapsing on her bedding instants later.

Catherine smiled, remembering the patient's advice. Let people see she was nice?

Yeah, right. That would work out.

She liked the girl, though. She was strong and resilient for a young one. A couple of days later, Cat helped her move back to the dorms. They waved at each other in the corridors over the next few weeks. Said hi, occasionally.

Catherine didn't know how it happened, exactly, but a lot more people seemed to speak to her these days. Asking for the time, just greeting her randomly, commenting about lessons.

She didn't mind.

The Return

End of May, Bash's phone buzzed around noon, a text from Chloe waking him up.

"Can you meet me at Levi's? I thought you'd be here."

He chuckled. He'd definitely spent way too much time on the hill.

"I'm at the dorm. Give me five minutes."

He brushed his teeth and took a quick shower before dashing up Night Hill. Chloe was in front of the mansion, her tall frame hidden behind piles of boxes.

"Moving in? Levi will be happy."

She snorted. "He wishes. That's just decorative stuff I ordered a while back for Cosnoc."

Bash whistled. "For Eirikr, you mean?"

As a huntsman, he'd always been fascinated by the elder vampire. Not only because he was the very first of their kind; he'd also created the huntsmen. Training humans and then spelling the strongest among them to become stronger, better, with a witch's brew colored with a drop of his blood. Back in his days, vampires had met no resistance, killing as they pleased. Eirikr had been the only one who wanted to do something about it. If not for him, the history of humanity might have been a lot different.

"I can run back and forth, but I figured I'd ask you to carry stuff with me, if you don't mind," she said carefully.

Bash was surprised. "Didn't Levi offer?"

Chloe chuckled. "He did. But I'm not ready to introduce those two. It'd be like my boyfriend meeting my father. Except my actual father is in prison, and this one is a psychotic elder vamp stuck in a cave. Anyway. I'll delay that for a little longer, if possible. But Eirikr asked about you. A huntsman turned vampire? He's interested."

Bash had to admit he was a little anxious, but he hid it well.

He grabbed three of the five large boxes and followed Chloe down Night Hill, through the path leading to the Institute, and then up Cosnoc, following the path to Eirikr's cave.

Bash had been on this hill several times. Jack organized races there, the occasional campfire, but they'd never gone anywhere near the caves.

As he approached, he felt a strange energy telling him to pull back. Leave.

"Ah, it hit you," said Chloe, turning to him. "Ignore it. It goes away with time. The witches who set up the spells around this place did a little bit to deter people from going in there, but they mostly concentrated on shields preventing Eirikr from coming out."

That made sense.

But as they walked farther down the dark path lined with overgrown trees, bushes, and long grass, Bash felt weak, lethargic. He started to pant. Every step seemed to cost him, making it harder to breathe. Then, the thirst started to distract him again.

He wasn't sure he would have been able to go that far before the change.

"Chloe? I don't think I can go much further."

He hated admitting weakness.

She frowned. "Really? We're not very far."

"It's..." He paused. "I could be wrong, but perhaps you're not affected because of your blood. Princess of the seven, Eirikrson, with divine nanocytes helping. You know. One of those things might make you less sensitive than the rest of us."

"Oh. Yeah, that makes sense. Shame. Let me get those boxes down, then I'll come back for the rest."

She returned less than a minute later, grinning.

"How's the psycho?"

"In good spirits. Although he would have liked to see you. Thanks for accompanying me, Bash."

"Don't mention it."

BASH HEADED OUT TO THE INSTITUTE'S COURTYARD, feeling awkward as shit. All eyes followed him as he walked toward Anika Beaufort, who was training Tris, Jack, Bat, Zavier, Easton, and Chris, students in the most advanced sparring class, which he'd once been a part of.

Bash inhaled deeply. Almost everyone in the court-yard smelled like fucking food. His friends were marginally better, but that wasn't saying much.

What the hell was he doing here?

But he knew. He hated it, but Cat's words from two weeks ago had stayed with him, bothering him enough that he was willing to try her way. If only to prove she was wrong. That the problem was more complicated than him simply not being used to the smell of human beings. Steven had told him they were monsters. The kid had lived with the curse for years, so he would know.

He needed a distraction. And suddenly he knew just what would do the trick.

A pair of lips on his. So fucking soft. A slender body under his palm. Slim, muscular legs around him. Shit, Catherine had felt so good.

His fists unclenched at his side and he took a calming breath, then crossed the yard. Thirst was now replaced by something else. Lust. But also annoyance.

She'd barely spared him a glance or said a word since that kiss. They patrolled in silence and went their separate ways at six every morning. And he hated it.

"Hey. You mind if I join?" he asked.

At least Anika was strong enough to stop him if he went off the rails. So was Jack, and maybe even Tris.

"While you haven't thought it necessary to grace us with your presence for fifteen weeks, you're still signed up for this class, Bash," Anika replied. "So please do, unless you want to flunk."

Oh. Yeah, he hadn't bothered to drop out of any of his old lectures. He wondered how pissed the rest of his teachers were.

"Sure. Cool. Erm—"

"I'll take you, big guy," Tris said with a wink, stepping away from her cousin. "Let's see if sprouting fangs has improved your footing."

He was grateful. Out of everyone except Anika and Jack, Tris was the least appetizing person here, and she could certainly take care of herself.

Though she hadn't turned yet, she was a born vampire. She'd always been faster than him, and stronger than most.

"All right. Today we're working with hands bound. You're expected to overthrow your opponent in three minutes or less. When you're in the role of the kidnapper, you are to imitate the fighting style of a sup —werewolf, witch, vamp, that's up to you. No huntsman techniques. We're practicing so that you know how to escape a sup holding you captive. Understood?"

Piece of cake, with his increased speed.

"To make the game fair, Jack, Tris, you have one minute. And Bash? You have fifteen seconds."

Shit.

Well, it was his fault for expecting Anika's class to be easy.

They took turns binding each other's wrists. Anika gave them iron bonds, while the other huntsmen worked with rope. Tris won, but it took her five minutes at first. Bash did manage to get her on her ass after a full minute. They kept alternating until they were both considerably better at moving despite the restraints. By the time Anika called the end of class, he'd improved to nineteen seconds, and Tris was at two and a half minutes.

"Not bad, sucker," she told him with a huge grin.

Then she wrapped her arms around him and squeezed hard. A little too hard for it to feel casual.

"I'm proud of you for being here," Tris said, before letting go.

Bash's throat tightened.

He wasn't proud as much as stunned and a little annoyed.

Two hours of sweating in the courtyard like the old days, and already he felt a difference. Smelled a difference.

Oh, they still smelled delicious beyond belief. But while he'd been concentrating on sparring, he'd somehow become a little more immune to the scent. He didn't think he was likely to jump on anyone right now. Unless they opened their wrist in front of him and start bleeding out.

He headed to his next class with Tris, wondering how pissed Professor Crane was going to be. The man took his leadership class seriously. A bear shifter businessman running a successful business in finance, he traveled to Oldcrest twice a week to teach, and he had little patience with slackers.

"You get along with the bear. Any advice?" Bash asked Tris, who snorted.

"Beg for his pardon? I swear his claws come out every time he glances at your seat."

Bash winced, stiffening as they approached the amphitheater.

Theo Crane, five foot ten, with salt-pepper

hair and arms the size of bolsters, growled low as soon as he saw him.

Tris passed him by, whispering, "Good luck."

Dammit. Bash approached the bear, hands behind his back.

"Good afternoon, sir."

"Is it now? Is that why you haven't bothered to attend class for thirteen weeks? Wasn't sunny enough for you?"

Bash didn't bother to point out that he'd been turned into a vampire. Any shifter could smell it, and any idiot would be able to note the difference in him. The stillness and pallor.

"My apologies, sir."

"Your apologies will not make up for almost four months of absence. A dissertation on pro-environmental behavior change using evidence-based practice might. I will have it on my desk before the summer holiday. Understood?"

Bash winced. In just under two weeks? Crane's leadership course was one of his most challenging classes. He was a huntsman; in his youth he'd studied creatures, combat, spells. He'd taken the basics in math and sciences, but that was about the extent of his education. Bash had a bachelor's in myths and legends. Economics, strategy, development, sustainability—that was like deciphering Chinese. Crane was a gifted orator, and while he wasn't exactly patient, his explanations were clear. Bash followed his lessons well enough. But if he was supposed to research those subjects himself, he might not be finished for months.

But he nodded. "Yes, sir."

"Very well. I trust you remember where your seat is, Sebastian."

He headed to his spot between Easton Read and Tris.

"East."

The man grunted, ill-humored. Bash didn't take it personally. Easton was always crotchety. His parents had died along with Bash's, but unlike him, Easton didn't have any siblings. He'd been twenty-two at the time, and alone. Few friends, no family. The huntsmen had tried to provide him with support, but he'd shut everyone out.

It probably didn't help that their parents' murderers had yet to be found.

They'd been on a mission to destroy Vlad, a vampire known for his savagery, so four of the best partners had been sent. Eight huntsmen against one. It should have been a piece of cake. But no one came back alive.

At twenty, Easton had come to the Institute to get his bachelor's, but since the incident, he'd changed. He had no ambition now. He'd said himself that he liked being a foot soldier, sent to kill things without having to worry about investigations or conspiracies. Bash was pretty certain he was back for his master's only because Vlad had stirred again, after more than a decade.

Six months ago, he'd massacred witches in London, members of Rose's Coven. The huntsmen reopened the investigation, but only fully licensed agents were allowed on the case. Bash got it. Vlad hadn't been caught yet, and the next time his name appeared on a mission, East wanted in.

Bash felt the same impulse when he'd first heard of Vlad's most recent antics. But then he'd remembered his brother and sister. His friends. And he'd decided to live.

He wondered what call he'd make now. He was stronger. Faster. And less attached to his existence.

An Unfamiliar Space

CHAPTER

14

The scent of the classroom was far worse than the courtyard, where the fresh air had diluted the smell of blood. Though the room was large, the smell was a lot more condensed, especially after Crane closed the door.

The first few breaths were hard. His fist tightened, and he trembled, concentrating just to remain seated. Part of him, the dark voice whispering at the back of his mind, was assessing the people around him, seeing them as prey.

The huntsmen's presence helped. Tris had a knife or two in her sleeve, and wouldn't hesitate to throw it at him if he messed up. That alone was enough to reel in the frustrated beast.

Bash opened his satchel and pulled out a blood bag. Then he stilled, realizing he was just opening the first out of twelve he stored in the refrigerated bag.

Damn.

He took a sip, and his shoulders dropped, his breathing deepened.

He could do this.

After a three-month break, suffering through Crane's lesson might have resulted in a headache if not for his new abilities. Instead, Bash found that his mind was soaking in every word and coming up with a thousand questions. And, unbelievably, forgetting about the thirst.

Dammit. He was going to have to thank Catherine fucking Stormhale and let her say a big fat "I told you so."

"Still good?" Tris asked him with a sunny smile as she put away her notebook.

Bash noted that he'd never bothered pulling his out. He remembered Crane's each and every word. Each graphic and date and number.

Somehow, his brain wasn't even exploding.

"Yeah, I'm fine."

"I have Literature. You?"

"Break until Spells tonight. I'll just go back to..." Levi's. He was about to say Levi's. His refuge. He could ask Chloe for news about her ancestor, and read another book, maybe train with someone. But after a moment, Bash decided against it. "The dorm."

He had an empty room he barely recognized, unpacked suitcases to sort out, and a life to rebuild.

Bash organized his stuff, dusting the top of his laptop before starting it up and signing in to the Institute's archives, a website he'd barely explored since the start of his studies. He'd only logged on to submit assignments to the professors who accepted electronic documents. The older immortals had a thing for paper.

He navigated awkwardly until he found Crane's

archives, then searched keywords related to his assignment and groaned. Dammit. There were thousands of pages. At least his reading speed had increased.

Bash flew through seven of the hundred and ninety-three documents containing the term "environment" before realizing that notes weren't the worst idea. He had a much better memory now, but the more he tried to store in his mind, the more jumbled and confusing everything became. He wrote down chapters and pages, and put the information right out of his consciousness, storing it in the list of things he could ignore. He was functioning like a computer, storing data on an external drive to avoid lag. A creepy notion, but now that he'd admitted it to himself, he found his task considerably easier.

Lifting his head to the window, Bash noticed that night had fallen. He looked at the time. Nine. After a moment of consideration, Bash set an alarm clock for eleven-thirty before returning to his task. It wouldn't do to miss his sentinel shift with Catherine.

Catherine Stormhale. She was always at the edge of his mind these days. When he thought about blood, he imagined her challenging him. When he didn't think about blood, he remembered that he owed that little bit of sanity to her. Bash saw she could easily become an obsession.

That kiss...

Yeah, he wasn't going there.

Bash's phone startled him, thankfully stopping his train of thought.

A video chat from Emilia.

"Hey, is everything all right?"

She didn't usually call out of the blue.

"Yep, I just wanted you to know that Paul has his first solo assignment."

Holy shit. That was big. Solo assignments were always easy, a quick trip down to the nearest coven to ask about a report of mistreatment. Nothing came of it, usually. But Bash remembered his. He'd been all red throughout the entire ordeal, his heart beating a thousand miles a minute.

As usual, Bash felt a mixture of pride in his brother and resentment that he couldn't be there when Paul returned.

But that was stupid. He wouldn't have been in Brighton even if he hadn't been bitten.

So, he just let go and smiled. Genuinely smiled at his sister.

"You look good, Sebastian. Anything happened?"

He shrugged. "I feel better, yeah. A little."

Emilia proved far too perceptive again. "It's a girl, isn't it?"

Bash groaned. "I'm twenty-eight, sister. I don't do girls."

"A woman, then. Vamp or huntsman? No, wait. It's a witch, right? Is that how you managed to do magic the other day?"

"There's no girl. No woman. No witch. I don't have time for—"

"Don't bother lying, I'll meet her this summer. Anyway, Paul's mission is tonight. Call him after ten, all right? And don't worry. I'll shadow him to make sure he doesn't get into any actual trouble."

Bash had to laugh. That was an unspoken tradition. Whenever a kid went on a first solo, one or two seasoned warriors followed discreetly. Bash's parents had trailed him at sixteen, then Bash and Jack trailed Emilia five years ago. She'd never needed them, but they would have been there if she had.

"I'm glad you're there for him."

"As you were there for me. I have to review my mission. Catch you later, Sebastian."

"Next weekend," he promised.

And for once, he might actually stay the entire weekend.

Might. He wasn't about to push himself and put his siblings in harm's way. But if he did improve over the next ten days, he could always try. As long as Luke was there to stop him in case he lost it.

Trust

Catherine was completely motionless, hand on the thick paper. She'd read the words five times, but they still stubbornly said the exact same thing. Words written by Drusilla's strange hand, in an early Latin alphabet.

There were only five of them.

Come home before summer break.

Simple and to the point. An order that she shouldn't have questioned.

Cat felt like her knees were going to give out.

An order to come home in less than three weeks.

The letter shouldn't have come as a surprise. It *didn't*. But the very idea made her feel sick. Weak. She couldn't imagine a worse fate than having to return to her golden cage and dance to her family's tune for the next few years. Not after Oldcrest. Not after tasting freedom and friendship.

Cat might have enjoyed her time here, but she didn't think she'd quite understood how much until now, when it was being taken from her.

Her fist tightened over the paper. She should be relieved. Drusilla wanting her out of the way meant that the Stormhales weren't part of this mess. That's what she'd thought at first.

But why before summer?

Many students remained in Oldcrest during the other breaks, but in July and August, barely anyone lived there, save for the permanent residents.

Anyone who wished to attack Oldcrest would benefit from doing it then. Did that mean her family was involved?

At the very least, they knew that something was going on and wanted to ensure Catherine wasn't there. She bit her lip.

Her duty to her family was written on her skin. Quite literally. She still had marks for every time she'd disobeyed. Scars. Her right knee had been broken once. Her wrist, a few times. Each of her fingers too.

Those punishments had been for minor offenses. If she defied Drusilla now, she knew the price would be far steeper.

It wasn't worth it. It just wasn't.

She was going home, and that was it.

Catherine bit her lip.

Then she rushed out of the dorms and ran right to Night Hill.

"Billevern."

The troll guarding the gates grunted at her. He didn't like her much, but he seemed to feel the same way about most people.

"Can I go through?"

Others had to state their purpose when they

wanted admittance to the hill, but Cat technically lived there.

He wordlessly pressed a button, and the brand-new gates barring the way tilted open.

"Thank you."

Cat thought about heading to Levi but decided against it. Instead, she stopped by the second house on the hill, right under hers.

"Anika? Anyone here?"

It was ten in the evening; she knew most of Anika's lessons were during the day, and her night shift started in two hours, same as Cat's. The woman appeared a few minutes later, wearing a kimono and fluffy sleepers.

"Hey! Nice of you to pop by. Fancy a drink?"

"It's not just a courtesy visit," she admitted. "I'm here because I have to tell someone. I think my family might be against us. Against Oldcrest."

Anika's brows lifted, and her jaw fell open.

"All right. Come in. I definitely need a drink for that conversation."

Cat walked in, following the professor through the beautiful gold and azure home modeled after Versailles.

No wonder. Anika's family was related to French royalty—the Bourbons and Beauforts were close cousins. Cat knew that most of her family still lived in the Loire Valley in a castle warded almost as well as the Institute.

Almost.

"How are they, by the way? Your family," Anika asked offhandedly, leading the way through the grandiose rooms.

Cat shrugged. "My brother texts occasionally. He's...well, he's Seth."

Anyone who'd ever met Seth would have understood.

Anika laughed. "No one was ever more aptly named. God of storm, chaos, disorder..."

Cat wished she could say something in defense of her elder brother, but the description fit—and given the fact that he had a was-scepter made for himself, he embraced the comparison.

"Well, he's causing chaos in Russia at the moment. Or was, last week."

"Good, good," Anika said.

They'd reached a large kitchen with copper pans and very sharp knives on display.

"And your sister?"

"We video chat," Cat said. "Not as often; she's still in Rome, and my family is keeping her busy. How about your siblings?"

"You know," the professor replied, opening a glass cabinet.

She pulled out a set of carved crystal martini glasses with a faint blue hue. Rather pretty, although a little too old-fashioned and girly for Cat's taste.

"What's your poison?"

Cat shrugged. "Anything, really."

"Come on, give me a challenge. I used to bartend for fun back in the day."

Now that was a surprise.

Every old vampire went through phases where their vocation felt tiresome, mundane. However much one might enjoy a task, doing it over and over for eternity sucked the passion out of it.

But a bartender? Cat wondered how many children of the seven ever did something so simple. She knew the Stormhales would never allow her to work in a bar.

But she and Anika were in very different positions. Cat was one of the youngest in her generation. Only five Stormhales were under a century old. Worse yet, she was the least powerful of those five. Anika was hundreds of years old and a master in combat. No one could tell her what to do.

Cat couldn't help a pang of envy.

"Surprise me."

"Ha! I knew I liked you. Take a seat."

She climbed on a barstool and watched Anika mix a drink with flair to show off her skills. Cat grinned as she watched the bottles fly, twist, and turn in the air and around Anika's hands.

"So, you were saying? About your family."

Cat bit her lip.

"Do you believe in coincidences?" she asked the professor.

"Another word for fate. Or schemes, depending on the situation."

She nodded. "Precisely. Well, how likely is it that half a dozen students start in the second semester, on the very same day and at the exact moment when the last Eirikrson enters the school?"

"A chance in a million," said Anika. "We discussed that in conclave the day before your arrival. Levi shut down the question. In hindsight, I'd say he was protecting Chloe."

She nodded. "Of course. But that doesn't change the fact that something—someone—sent us all here.

The air witch," she said, pausing to recall her name. "Gwen. The fox. Maybe even the huntsman."

Cat wished she'd attended orientation with them, but she had arrived too late.

"And me," she added. "I think that our arrival had something to do with Chloe."

"More than likely. For good or ill."

Cat remained silent. But really, who would believe that whatever scheme her family was concocting could be conceived as good?

"What makes you think that the Stormhales are against Oldcrest?"

Cat pulled the letter out of her pocket and handed it to Anika. In exchange, Anika gave her a drink that smelled fruity and delicious. Cat detected raspberry, pineapple, maybe peach. Definitely vodka. Something else too.

She brought it to her lips and moaned in delight. What was that?

She wanted to ask, but instead she concentrated on the point at hand. Her mind often betrayed her, distracted by random irrelevant details. This was too important to let her mind wander.

"Drusilla tells me to return home before summer. That's very specific. And I was supposed to go back regardless. This feels like...a warning. Like they know something is about to happen. I want to warn the others, I think. I could be exaggerating. Maybe there's a party I'm supposed to attend. But something feels off. What do you think?"

Cat had gone to Anika for advice because the woman was as smart as she was powerful. Plus, she was a lot more than just a professor. As an ancient Beaufort, she had as many slayers and spies as Levi in her service. She must at least suspect something, or know for sure that her family wasn't involved.

"I think," Anika said carefully, "that you're much smarter than your aunt gives you credit for. Unfortunate, really. I liked you."

Cat froze an instant before her vision started to blur.

She looked down at her drink and gasped.

So very sweet. So very fruity. Just enough to mask a faint scent she hadn't recognized.

Bane

A coppery hint, with a touch of fermented flesh, like rotten blood. Nightbane. The one poison that could affect their kind.

If the poison hadn't been mixed with anything, Cat would have recognized it a mile away, but mingled with so many scents and served by someone she trusted? She had suspected nothing.

Cat tumbled to her feet, falling forward on her knees. Head down, she did her best to cough it up, in vain.

"Oh, chill, sweetheart," Anika said casually.

She lifted her head, and from the corner of her blurring vision, saw the professor smiling down at her, tilting her head.

"Your blood isn't mine to spill. That was just a drop to keep you nice and quiet while I send a little note to Drusilla."

Fuck. Fuck. Fuck.

How stupid was she? She knew there was an

enemy, someone informing the queen, or whoever was against them. Why hadn't she stopped to think that it could be Anika? Because she'd known her before the Institute. Because she was old, wise, and had the right name. Because she had turned soft and trustful.

What an idiot.

Anika was writing a letter on her breakfast table to Cat's aunt. And if that letter reached Drusilla, she was as good as dead. The Stormhale clan didn't allow for many mistakes in general, but there was one price for treason. Death. A painful, public execution, so gruesome it would be spoken of for the next hundred years.

Time. She had to play for time.

One drop of nightbane would run its course, leave her system, and she could fight back. Stop the letter. Stop Anika. Warn...who? Who did she trust?

To her surprise, even in light of this betrayal, names flooded the edge of her confused mind.

Chloe. Levi. Greer. Even Billevern would help now.

"Sebastian," she whispered.

That this particular name would come to mind, let alone escape her lips, confused her. She didn't even know him, so why would she trust him with something so very important—her life? But her instincts were clear.

She had to get to one of them, any of them.

"It's not your fault, you know. Your aunt is a power-hungry bitch. A smart woman would have brought you up to speed, given you a clear mission. Sending you here without a word and expecting you to just comply? That wasn't fair. Still, I can't let you get in the way."

"Why?" Cat croaked, her throat hurting.

She didn't think it had ever been quite so dry. Cat hadn't felt sick once since being turned. But now, her stomach was convulsing, churning, burning.

"Why? Because bitch or not, Drusilla has a fucking point. We don't want the Eirikrsons to return. Especially not one who's decades away from spreading her legs and spouting out little De Villiers. They're going to take what is rightfully ours. Power."

Her head was spinning. Cat wanted to drop to the ground and just rest. But if she did that, she'd be gone.

She had to keep Anika talking. Time was her best defense now.

"Do you think...Drusilla," she managed to mumble, "will share power?"

Anika shrugged. "It's a big world. I'm fine just keeping a country or two."

She couldn't believe her ears. This was Anika. Anika, who wasn't with her pompous family in France because she preferred teaching students over sitting in a palace.

Catherine started to understand her mistake. Anika wasn't here because she wanted to be a professor.

She was here because she wanted to live on Night Hill. The only seat of power truly recognized by all.

Anika disgusted Cat. Truly, to the bottom of her heart. Cat clung on to that feeling—the pure rage, fury, revulsion—and let it fuel her. Keep her awake.

She managed to get to her knees.

"Drusilla will...use you. And spit you out."

Cat started to feel better. The tremor was stopping. The pain around her abdomen receded.

"Drusilla is bound by her oath as well as any of us. She promised me France, Germany, and Spain, and I shall have them."

"What about the queen, then?" Cat pushed, hoping for answers.

If she lived through today, she needed to know as much as possible.

Anika snorted. "That upstart is an idiot. Ambitious, I'll give you that. But an idiot nonetheless. She doesn't have enough support to achieve her goal. And while Chloe and Tom breathe, she can't even use her one real source of power."

The professor knew a lot more than she, a lot more than all of them. She needed to keep her talking without realizing that Cat was interrogating her.

Cat decided to do what she did best, a strategy that generally worked with ancient vampires, who often underestimated youth. She played dumb.

"You mean Chloe is stopping the queen? That doesn't make any sense."

But it did. She perfectly understood what Anika had hinted at.

The so-called queen was drawing power from the Eirikrsons, power that she'd managed to steal from them while no one could access it. Now that the true heirs were back, she was cut off from it.

Which could only mean one thing. The queen had been turned by an Eirikrson.

"The two petulant children may not use Skyhall, but you know what's buried inside. The same thing festers under your house, here on the hill."

Cat nodded.

When all seven founder lines turned against Eirikr,

they used dark magic to seal him in his tomb on Cosnoc, the forbidden hill. Magic that had cost a lot more than a few coins tossed at a parlor-trick witch.

Blood.

The strength of the seven families' blood kept Eirikr imprisoned. The spell had not faded through the ages because the blood anchoring it still lay under the tomb.

The beating hearts of the seven strongest among their kind.

The purpose of the sacrifice had been to seal Eirikr, but soon, the seven noticed that their strength increased while in their house.

As did their cruelty. Their rage. Their darkness.

Every family soon moved away. Save for Levi, Anika, and Alexius.

Cat used to believe that was because they were strong enough to withstand the pull of the evil presence. Now she wasn't so sure.

Something tapped at the window, and Anika let in a large eagle.

"I think that's quite enough chitchat, don't you?"

She rolled her note and placed it in the bird's claw.

"Yes. I think so, too," Cat replied, eyes on the window.

She was no Seth. She was no Drusilla. Her power was minimal. Inconsequential.

But for better or worse, she was a Stormhale, and she'd be damned if she let a treacherous bitch ruin her life.

Cat called to the sky with everything she had, everything she was. She called to the blood under her house and the clouds overhead. She even called to the waters of the lake, though they'd never answered her before. She dug deep inside her, emptying her mind of everything, everyone, except the one thing that mattered in the end.

Power.

The Traitress

The whisper had been clear in the night. So very clear. Bash felt like Catherine had been saying his name right against his ear. Her deep accent, rolling each syllable around her tongue, was unmistakable.

It was a dream. Just a dream. There was nothing peculiar about a man dreaming about a sexy woman's voice. Particularly a few weeks after kissing said woman.

But he heard something unsettling in that voice. Something that bothered him. He couldn't place his finger on what, but he was uneasy.

Cat had said his name a handful of times, perhaps, but it never sounded like this. Almost a plea.

Just a fantasy, he reasoned. Nothing more.

Bash had half an hour until his shift southwest of the territory. He was almost done tidying up his last bullet point on his report when he felt the change in the air. The damn ground shook underneath the dorm.

But it was more than that. A force was *exploding*. Shattering.

Next, he saw a flash of light through the dark skies and thunder resounded in the distance.

He was out of the dorm before his next heartbeat, and halfway up the hill within ten seconds.

The lightning had hit the second house on the hill, destroying part of the roof.

Bash rushed to the front door moments before two women burst out of a window. Cat first, kicked back under Anika's heel.

Anika's right side was scorched, her skin burned black and her clothes in rags.

What the hell?

Bash rushed to Cat's side, helping her up to her feet.

"Are you all right?"

Moments later, he felt Levi and Chloe approach. Then Mikar, and Alexius. The uproar had caught everyone's attention.

"I caught her writing to her stinking family," Anika screeched, pointing to the large bird of prey flying away from the house.

Bash felt Cat freeze completely. She wasn't even breathing. Her eyes were the picture of shock. And fear.

"She's betraying us. Sending them secrets by air so they can't be intercepted. When I confronted her, she attacked me."

Levi took one step forward, until he'd reached Bash and Cat, his gaze cold.

Bash didn't even think. He placed himself between

her and the two-thousand-year-old monster. The predator who could kill him without breaking a sweat.

Levi watched Cat without a word. Bash glared at him.

"Mikar. Ruby," the ancient called.

Ruby. He'd heard that name before; Levi and his employees mentioned her occasionally. One of Levi's slayers who worked around the territory. She wasn't very social, though.

But now that he'd called her, she appeared in the distance, like she'd been standing close by all along.

Ruby had dark hair, light brown skin, and was dressed in ancient white rags. She looked like a ghost. If ghosts could drink the blood of their enemy and bathe in mud.

Bash stilled himself, ready to fight against one, or both if necessary. They were not going to hurt Cat without hearing her out, dammit. And she wasn't in a condition to speak right now, that much was obvious. She smelled wrong. She looked weak.

But when the slayers moved, they fell on Anika instead.

Bash breathed out. Cat didn't. She was trembling, watching the whole thing with wide eyes, her breathing shallow, unfocused.

Anika was one of the best fighters Bash had ever seen in action; there was a reason why she taught the immortals and huntsmen at the Institute. Though his attention mostly remained on Cat, Bash followed the scene from the corner of his eye.

Anika had one knife in each fist, and she was ferocious with both, anticipating all of Mikar's moves.

Mikar was just fast enough to avoid her deadly blades. Then Ruby joined the fray.

She wasn't like Mikar, or Levi, or Jack—or any fighter Bash had ever seen. There was no grace, no elegance to her style.

She was fast as the wind, light as a feather, and ferocious as any beast.

Anika would have won against Mikar. Might have won against Ruby. She had no chance against both.

Ruby didn't mind the knives. She didn't care about being kicked or punched or bitten. While Mikar kept Anika's blades occupied, Ruby went for the throat, planting her fangs deep inside Anika's neck and holding still. A warning. If Anika so much as moved, Bash knew the slayer would rip it open.

"You're okay?" Levi asked Cat, softly.

Cat wasn't moving or saying anything just now. Bash got it; she was in shock. He remembered his own sister after they'd been told about their parents.

So he did the same thing he'd done with Emilia back then: wrapped his arms around her shoulders and pulled her close.

She allowed it, for a moment.

Then she pushed against him, shaking her head and closing her eyes.

"What's wrong with her?" Chloe asked, rushing to Cat's side.

"I think she's in shock."

"No—well, perhaps, but that's not the primary concern," Alexius said. "Her eyes are red, wide, and unfocused. Nightbane? Nod if that's the case."

Cat bobbed her head once.

"The—" she tried, then cleared her throat. "The letter."

Bash looked up. Even in the darkness, he could see that a bird—an eagle?—was flying away.

He frowned. For her to say that now, when every word was taxing, the message must be important. Crucial. Bash saw tears at the corners of her eyes.

Dammit. What could he do? He'd never felt this hopeless.

The wind picked up in the south, and loud, high-pitched screams came from the Institute. He glanced at the building and found it wrapped in darkness. Fast-moving darkness. Frowning and focusing on the shadows, he saw wings. Hundreds and hundreds of black wings.

The ravens used as messengers in Oldcrest.

All eyes went to Chloe, who was focusing on the eagle, her bright blue eyes narrowed in on her target.

No one was surprised when she dissolved into mist a moment later, her body and soul syncing with her beasts. Her familiars.

No raven could outrun a bird of prey, or would ever attack one. Right now, the ravens were Chloe Eirikrson.

She flew through the sky as fast as any storm, and the next cry piercing the night belonged to the poor eagle.

Bash winced on its behalf.

The ravens returned to the hill in a cloud of shadow, and Chloe reappeared in front of them, holding the brown and white bird carefully but firmly.

Cat almost collapsed against Bash. He wrapped an arm around her waist, supporting her as she stood.

"There, there, beautiful thing," Chloe murmured, her voice a soft caress so very soft.

Her tone had changed, soft as silk, sweet as honeysuckle.

Bash immediately felt like stepping closer, asking how he could be of assistance.

Kneeling.

Levi said Chloe was a whisper. He never understood what that meant, and the explanation hadn't really helped.

"Whispering is a very rare skill," Mikar had told him. "It's a form of mind control that can't be learned; you're either born with it or you aren't."

Chloe hadn't liked that very much. "I control people? No way!"

"It's part of who you are. Accept it so you can learn to control it. When you want something, you'll ask for it, but we won't be able to stop ourselves from obeying." The slayer had shrugged. "Well, I can resist it now. It won't affect Levi or other ancients either. But with each passing year, you're likely to get stronger."

Bash was no ancient, and he could *feel* her influence, her power pouring over him like a comforting silk wrap. Even knowing what it was, he wanted to give in.

Bash started to move, and felt Catherine shift against his torso, bracing herself to stand without his support.

He snapped right out of it.

Chloe removed the letter tied to the bird's leg, then opened it and read, "To D. Storm. Your youngest's loyalties are questionable. Send an extraction party immediately. A."

She snorted and glared at Anika, who was still restrained by both slayers, before handing the bird to Greer.

"You lying piece of filth."

Alexius had stayed away until then, but now he approached Cat, taking her wrist to check her pulse.

"Nightbane poisoning, I believe. Blood and rest," he prescribed. "You'll be fine after some sleep. Someone will have to cover your shift."

"And mine," Bash added. "I'll look after her."

Cat didn't protest, which attested to her state.

"How—" Her voice sounded so fucking weak. She cleared her throat and tried again, looking up to Levi. "How did...know?"

Then Bash understood her silence, as well as her shock.

It wasn't just the nightbane. She hadn't expected them to trust her. Choose her over Anika.

Bash felt unreasonably angry.

Levi snorted, as though the question amused him.

"Because whoever you were before Oldcrest, whatever you've done, you want to belong here."

Needs

C at closed her eyes, feeling more exhausted by the second now that she felt like it was safe to rest.

Chloe got the letter. It hadn't reached Drusilla. She was going to be okay.

After one or two years of sleep.

"Are you sure she's all right?" Chloe demanded.

Cat forced a smile that didn't reassure anyone, given their expressions. She held her thumb up. "I'm peachy," she promised. "I just need to rest my head."

Then she realized she didn't have a year at all. She could only afford a nap at most. Then, she would have to speak to them.

There were Stormhale secrets that she could no longer afford to keep. Not now. Anika had been plotting with her family, sure, but who else? Drusilla might still get a note about her by the end of the day despite Chloe stopping this one.

Which meant that protecting Oldcrest wasn't just

about her friends, or a matter of right and wrong. It was about survival.

"Come on, let's go."

She didn't protest, letting Sebastian lead her down the hill toward the dorms. As they passed Billevern's barrier, the troll growled low.

"What's wrong with her?" he asked, somewhat threateningly.

Sebastian was wise enough to reply promptly. Angering a troll was nothing short of suicidal.

"She was drugged. Alexius says she needs rest and blood, that's all."

The troll nodded before glaring down at her. "You get better, understood?"

She laughed, even though it hurt her lungs and abs.

"I'll try, Billevern."

"It's Bill. And boy, moving's hurting her. Help the girl, you idiot."

He laughed. "Well, we'd better listen to Bill. Arms around my neck, okay?"

Cat grimaced but did as she was told, if only because this was the first time the troll had given her the time of day. She didn't want him to be pissed at her.

Sebastian carried her like a princess.

Oh.

That was kind of nice. And she liked his smell.

No, she *adored* his smell. It was like chocolate and spice mixed with rum and sprinkled with strawberry.

Cat bit down on her lip. Shit, Alexius hadn't been kidding. She seriously needed blood, right now, before she sank her teeth right inside his neck.

That wasn't unusual between vampires. Intense,

intimate? Yes. But not unusual. Cat had never done it, but she knew that lovers, mates, husbands and wives exchanged blood. Craving vampire blood was different, though—the sort of thing that only happened to ferals. Or Eirikrsons.

She looked down to her lap. She had no business wanting to drink from Sebastian, regardless of how good he smelled or how weak she felt.

"You can let me down now," she said when they approached the dorm.

Sebastian snorted.

"Right. Do you know what Billevern would do to me if he hears that? Even Levi is careful with that man."

She bit back a groan, then held her breath, keeping her gaze away from his neck. Bash's celerity was greatly appreciated. They were in front of her bedroom within seconds.

"Keys?"

"It's open," she replied.

He pushed the handle down and whooshed past the door.

Cat blushed. Shit. She hadn't expected company.

Her room, here or in Rome, was her den, the one place where she could relax, chill out with music blasting in her ears without caring about what anyone thought of her.

And it was chaos. But she could find any book in the stack on the floor. Sure, half of her wardrobe was piled up in the room rather than folded or hung, but the clothes on her armchair were dirty and those on her bench just had to be ironed. An organized mess, in short.

A gentleman may have remained silent.

"Jesus, did a tornado hit or something?"

She wasn't strong enough to laugh, but she did manage to punch his shoulder. A pathetic hit.

He gently put her down on her bed.

"Blood?" he asked.

She pointed to her fridge in the corner of the room.

"There's a microwave..." A yawn interrupted her speech. "Somewhere."

Her eyes closed, not opening again until dawn, though falling asleep took a moment.

Long enough for her to wonder whether she'd ever slept with anyone quite so close. Even her brother. Even her sister.

She must have been quite tired, because she faded out of consciousness without even thinking about telling Sebastian to leave.

❧

CAT WAS NO STRANGER TO PAIN, BUT SHE COULDN'T recall ever having a headache quite as acute, like someone had lit a fire at the base of her skull.

That was nothing to the furnace burning her throat. Thirst like she'd never known. Thirst so strong she wanted to sink her teeth into the first thing, the first person, she could hunt down.

Her eyes opened. She didn't need a mirror to know they were bright silver. The eyes of a hunter focusing on the thing right in front of her.

A glass filled with blood.

She moved faster than she ever had, knocked some

of it onto her bed, and didn't care one bit. Her eyes closed as she gulped the blood down, moaning in relief.

It tasted...wrong. Stale. Disgusting.

Cat opened her eyes again and found Bash sitting on her office chair, which he'd dragged next to her bed.

He had another glass at the ready.

"I called Alexius when you crashed without drinking. He said you'd be parched when you woke up. I can relate."

Cat gratefully took the second glass and downed it too, though a little slower this time. It still tasted rancid.

Blood was like water to her. Tasteless, simple. Necessary. She didn't like or dislike it, she just...needed it to survive. Her palate wasn't so refined as to prefer one blood type over another. They were all the same, a liquid she couldn't survive without.

Right now, everything she knew was flipped on its head. And she realized what an ass she'd been.

Her eyes cut to Sebastian. He still smelled so very good. As tempting as an apple pie right out of the oven.

"Sorry. I was a bitch," she said with a wince.

"On which occasion?" Sebastian asked.

Cat snorted, or laughed; she couldn't quite tell.

"When I implied you were weak. For needing blood the way you do," she added.

She'd believed that since she was a newborn, turned only twelve months ago, she could remember what he was going through quite clearly. But if tonight was any indication, she had no idea. And no wonder.

All her life, she'd known she would eventually turn into a vampire. And she'd been told what to expect, and trained to control her thirst. The conditioning had started early. When she'd been thirsty as a child, she'd had to wait an hour before being given a drop of water. In her teens, she'd fasted for days on end, all the while sparring. Assuming that she could understand what someone like Bash felt upon turning had been self-centered as hell.

This was her first time experiencing bloodlust in twelve months. And she wasn't dealing with it well.

The Challenge

Something was wrong with Catherine, and Bash fucking hated it.

He wanted to ask, but knew she'd just tell him to bugger off.

"You had a point, by the way," he said, mostly to distract her. "What you said worked. My thirst is getting better with some exposure to human scent. I *was* avoiding the issue."

"Sure, but if your thirst is anything like this, I get why you'd want to."

Ah. She was desperate for blood. He certainly could relate to that.

"More blood?"

She'd just finished her second glass, but she shut her eyes and shook her head.

"No, this isn't helping. It tastes awful, and isn't even taking the edge off." She sighed. "I just need to keep it under control."

Bash watched her with rapture, impressed and frustrated all at once.

He'd been trained as a fucking warrior and couldn't handle the thirst. Here she was, just wishing it away.

"Have you ever drunk from someone's vein?" Bash found himself asking.

Her eyes flew open.

She looked a lot better than she had four hours ago when she'd fallen asleep. But her eyes were still silver, not their usual blue.

"Of course not."

"I have. I think that's one of the reasons why I'm like this. Unsatisfied." He paused. "Chloe fed me from her wrist that day, after I'd been bitten. She had to, to save me. But the bags of blood I drink—they're nothing compared to the real thing. If you haven't tried that, well, there's no way you'd know."

Plus, there was the fact that he'd been bitten by a feral, not a regular vampire.

"Ignorance doesn't excuse cruelty," Catherine retorted. "At least it shouldn't. Just take my apology and let's call it a night."

He laughed. "All right. Apology accepted. Now, how do you feel?"

"Okay," she replied. "I have my strength back. The thirst will go, in due time." She winced, admitting, "And it would help if I didn't have anyone with fresh blood around me right now."

He certainly understood that.

Bash nodded. "All right. Then I'll go back to work."

It was only one in the morning; he could still replace whoever had covered his shift.

"Sure thing. I'll see you tonight."

Leaving wasn't easy. He didn't like closing the door

behind him. Her scent had been all around the room, and he'd loved every bit of it. The fresh air was so very boring to him, without the hints of vanilla and seaside.

He headed south and found Mikar patrolling with the frightening, elusive vampire he'd seen earlier. Ruby.

"Hey."

"How is she?" the barbaric woman asked.

Bash was surprised she spoke at all, let alone in English. He couldn't quite place her thick accent. Old Scottish, perhaps, or maybe Irish. Something lost a long time ago.

"Well enough," he replied, then paused. "Thirsty. I think my presence wasn't helping."

Mikar and Ruby exchanged a glance that seemed knowing; they understood thirst so strong they wanted to drink from fellow vampires.

Bash wondered how many among their kind experienced it. Maybe it was a lot more common than what he'd believed.

"It'll fade in time. The girl has courage. If she's in trouble, you come to me," Ruby ordered.

Bash nodded, and she walked away, heading toward the Wolvswoods.

"Don't take it personally. She doesn't like people much."

Bash laughed. "Who am I to talk?"

He'd avoided most of his friends for months.

Mikar glanced at him. "You seem to be doing better."

"Yes." Thanks to Catherine. "I'm getting used to the smell. Or, rather, distracting myself by ignoring it. My brain is so weird. Unfamiliar."

"It's still your mind. It's just been improved. Think of it as though you just added hardware to an existing computer. Maybe you upgrade the disk or the memory, but it still has the same files, the same operating system."

"Just faster," Bash added. "And with different limits."

Mikar nodded. "Exactly. But you can run new programs now."

He thought back to what Chloe had done earlier. Bash had seen Levi appear and disappear in a cloud of mist and thought nothing of it because he was Levi. Old, powerful, larger than life. But seeing Chloe, who'd been turned alongside him, vanish and inhabit birds like that? It only emphasized the extent of his ignorance about his new body and mind.

"I *should* learn," he said carefully. "I want to learn how to *operate* the new system. Not just to control my thirst. I want to know how to sync with animals, read minds. Use magic if I can. This...thing I've become. It's me. And it doesn't have to be evil. It doesn't even have to be useless."

Mikar chuckled. "Syncing, telepathy, magic? That's not quite three-month-old level. And some never acquire one skill, let alone three."

Bash shrugged. "Might as well aim high. However long it takes."

"Right. Well, I can't help with any of the magic stuff. It's never been my inclination," the slayer told him. "But I can teach you one thing."

"What?"

Mikar grinned. "Your limits. I'm going to give you thirty seconds. No more, no less. Then you'll run from the train tracks back to the Wolvswoods, over and over again, until the end of our shift at six. I will follow that exact path for the next five hours. And if I catch you, I will drink from you until you're at the very brink of death. You may survive, but you will suffer. For days, you will suffer. Your thirst will get a thousand times worse."

Bash blinked, confused. How the fuck was that supposed to be helpful?

"That sounds like a terrible idea. Can we, like, not do that?"

"Thirty. Twenty-nine. Twenty-eight."

Shit. They were doing it.

Bash dashed south as fast as his immortal limbs could carry him, and then faster. Twenty-seven seconds later, he felt the air shift. Something was following. Something big. Strong.

You may survive.

Fuck. Fuck. Fuck.

He ran faster. His limbs hadn't hurt that way since before he turned. His lungs burned and his breathing was ragged—too fast, too hectic.

But he ran all the same, even when his body begged for a break, even when he felt sick.

That was when he realized one thing. He wanted to live. Two weeks ago, he hadn't been so sure, but now, he was desperate to stay alive.

The sun rose in the distance. Six was drawing near, but his body was betraying him. The predator behind him was closing in.

Fuck. He growled as he pushed for one last sprint. He had this. Until six.

He could do this.

"Hey!"

Bash stopped. Tris was standing in front of him.

He glanced back, seeing Mikar approaching in the distance.

"What are you doing here?" he asked, eyes wide.

He didn't want her in the way when the ancient drew near.

"What are *you* doing here?" Tris echoed. "It's seven. My shift started an hour ago."

He blinked.

What?

Bash bent forward, holding his knees and breathing hard.

He didn't look at Mikar but felt him approaching all the same.

Why hadn't the ass told him they were past the time? Damn him.

He didn't have the strength to rant. Instead, he simply cut to the chase. "I hate you."

A Curse

When Cat woke up, she immediately headed to the Institute, walking right to the tower the vampires had claimed for their studies. More often than not, only Levi and Alexius occupied the tower. Today, Fin Varra was there too, lounging on a chaise.

"I'm sorry to interrupt."

"By all means, please interrupt," Fin said. "I was listening to a dreadfully dull little story."

Her eyes went from the vampires to the fae, but she decided their conflict was none of her business. She had enough problems of her own right now.

Cat explained everything Anika had revealed about the queen, and her potential affiliation to the Eirikrsons.

"I could be wrong, but I believe there two distinct threats. The queen, and the other families," she concluded.

Levi nodded. "Thank you, Catherine. That was helpful. And it fits in with what I know."

She had other things to say, but she knew she was dismissed. Levi was visibly concerned, so she left the tower, walking down the hundreds of stairs in a flash.

Then her suffering started.

Cat kept her fists, jaw, and teeth clenched through each lesson, feeling like a bomb about to explode. There was one thing on her mind. Just one. Blood.

Worse yet, she didn't even want the blood of anyone around her. Her classmates, her professors, the men and women in the cafeteria all smelled like the most boring bag of O-positive.

She had other prey in mind.

Bash.

What the hell was wrong with her? A fellow vampire shouldn't be that fucking tempting.

"Hey," Greer greeted her at the start of her alchemy class.

She assisted Professor Helsing, who'd made it down from the tower faster than her.

"You're good?"

Cat nodded. She wasn't quite lying, but she was also stretching the truth a bit.

"Let's see how much your brewing technique has improved in the last week, shall we?" Alexius challenged at the start of class. "We're going to work on a healing brew. You'll decant essence of solanaceae first, for a painless anesthetic, then prepare a seven-step salve. You'll find the list on your desk. Two hours. This is practice, but it will likely be on your end-of-year testing."

Shit. Of course they were working on one of the most important potions now, when she was distracted.

On a day when everything passed as a vague blur,

this lesson was just a little bit clearer, mainly because she could see Alexius glaring at her and Greer shooting her worried looks every now and then.

She should have stayed in her room. Slept it off. She'd need someone's notes anyway.

Cat butchered the healing drought, doubling the nightshade content and adding way too much crushed spider.

"That's not bad," Alexius said.

She looked up, surprised. He was holding the dark blue mixture in the air, observing it in the fading afternoon light.

"Really?"

"I mean, it would kill most creatures the moment it entered their lips, of course. But creating poisons quite that efficient is no small feat."

Cat groaned. She'd definitely have to study this one before summer.

Cat was here for her MBA in charms and spells. She'd picked that subject because magic was her weakness. She wasn't an accomplished elemental mage, so that degree would mean a lot. To her, at least. She wasn't foolish enough to believe that it would matter to her family.

Now she second guessed her choice. She didn't like potions at all. She hadn't enjoyed chemistry in her youth, and that was no different.

"Sorry, I'm—" thirsty. Out loud, she opted for, "distracted."

"You can take an extra class on Saturday morning at ten o'clock. Greer is supervising."

Cat nodded. Whether she liked the class or not, she had no intention of flunking.

"In the meantime, I think I will take this one. You never know when having a poison in your sleeve will be useful."

Was Alexius teasing her about the previous night? She couldn't quite tell. He always looked like he was making fun of everyone, anyway.

"I promise I'll pay attention if you ever cover antidotes."

The vampire grimaced. "What's the fun in that?"

Some women giggled at the back of the room. Of course they did. A large percentage of Oldcrest's female population had a crush on Alexius. The other half would probably do him anyway. Had *probably* done him.

Alexius was around seven hundred years old, young enough to understand this day and age, old enough to know how to use all of his bloodline's devastating power. Cruel enough to find it fun. Cat couldn't say she knew much about him, but she'd heard the rumors. Every child of the seven had a reputation. Alexius's sin was having a completely screwed-up moral compass. Murder was his solution to most problems. When he couldn't slash a throat, he paid someone to do it for him. Even his family, renowned for doing just that for centuries, had enough of his antics. He didn't respect alliances, often went back on his word, and would have betrayed his own mother if it suited his purposes.

So they cursed him. Paid a coven to tether him to Oldcrest, where he couldn't do much harm.

Of course, regular humans, witches who hadn't been involved, and shifters had no clue about all that.

They only knew him as a hot prince with a wicked smile and a vampire's appetite for depravity.

Levi held monthly parties at his place, as was expected of him. The conclave and a select few were welcome to attend. But Alexius's weekly parties were open to just about anyone with a short skirt and firm breasts.

Basically, he was a twenty-year-old frat boy in a body hotter than sin. A dangerous combination. Cat didn't blame her classmates for their infatuations. Hell, she might even have fallen for him herself if she hadn't been harder to impress.

She knew prettier men. Stronger ones. More powerful ones. While her standards weren't very high when it came to her bedmates—she liked them handsome enough to look at and skilled with their extended limbs—she'd never been fond of megalomaniacs.

The last few days had changed her opinion of him. Some. Seeing him work on Maddy had been mindblowing, and it raised questions. Who was he? The agile, confident healer who knew everything about patching up a human, or the careless, carefree, indifferent man she'd heard about?

Cat didn't think she had the time or inclination to find out. After Anika, she vowed to stay away from anyone who struck her as untrustworthy.

Potions was her last lesson of the day. She had five hours off, and then her sentinel shift.

Earlier today, Cat had received a raven asking whether she was fit to serve, and she'd immediately sent back a yes. Now, she half regretted it. Not because of the shift itself—the distraction couldn't hurt. But because she was supposed to work with him.

Sebastian.

Fuck, why was his scent driving her so crazy? Cat rushed to her dorm and lay on her bed, eyes closed. And through her mind's eye, she saw him. His neck, his veins. Imagined herself biting it. *Licking* it.

She closed her eyes and breathed in and out. She could control this. She *would* control this.

But she'd never open her mouth to criticize anyone's lack of restraint again.

She headed back to her room and locked herself in, concentrating on her breathing until she felt a little more in control.

An Intruder

CHAPTER
21

Bash was not looking forward to another night running from the psychotic slayer. Mikar had seemed like an all-right dude until that morning, but he was clearly deranged. Or sadistic. Possibly both.

He'd stumbled into his bedroom and crashed for so long he missed his combat class. Which wasn't the worst thing, given that they no longer had a teacher.

He was in good form the next morning, his muscles having healed overnight. A definite improvement over his previous life. Back when he'd been a huntsman, he would have felt a six-hour run for days, if not weeks.

Working with Mikar again sounded like something right out of a nightmare, so he should have been relieved when he spotted the stubborn and beautiful blonde vamp at the edge of the Wolvswoods close to midnight. Instead, he rushed to her side and snapped, "What the *hell* are you doing here, Stormhale?"

She rolled her eyes. "My shift."

Bash narrowed his eyes. "You were poisoned just three days ago. With nightbane," he said, like she might have forgotten.

"So?" Cat seemed amused. "We're vampires. If something doesn't kill us, we sleep it off."

He knew that, but he didn't think he'd completely understood just how fast they healed, how different their bodies were, until waking up today. He had no cramps, no aches, no muscle spasms after being chased by Mikar. It made sense that she'd healed too, although poison didn't compare to a marathon.

Bash sighed. "You didn't look okay that day. You weren't just hurt. You were...anxious."

And out of control. He chose not to point that out.

Catherine glared at him, and he could guess exactly what she was thinking—that he had no business sticking his big nose into her affairs. But all she said was, "We'd better start our patrol, don't you think?"

He nodded stiffly before walking in silence by her side.

It was a comfortable sort of silence, and this time, whenever she stopped, he didn't have to ask why. He followed her gaze to watch the stars. Rabbits. Wolves.

Wait, wolves?

Catherine inclined her head in a greeting that didn't feel warm or welcoming. But it did show respect. Bash imitated her, and the three wolves watching them from the shadows glanced at each other.

The black wolf in front, taller than the others, and broader too—was clearly the alpha. A gray wolf stood at his right, considerably thinner but no smaller. To the left was a beautiful beast with reddish fur that might have been a coyote.

"The pack who live in the woods?" Bash asked.

"Yes, I think so. It's no wonder that they'd wonder what's going on, if Levi hasn't told them yet."

Bash didn't know much about these werewolves. Jack had mentioned them once or twice, saying that they were one of the oldest packs in the world. Whatever that meant. He was just surprised that they were content to live here in Oldcrest, although werewolves were territorial. Living near so many witches, vampires, and even shifters from other packs couldn't be easy.

"Maybe he should bring them up to speed," Bash mused out loud.

Cat snorted. "It's not quite that simple. I heard he invited them to the last conclave. They didn't show. Werewolves are..."

The black beast bared his teeth, growling a warning.

Now wasn't the time to insult werewolves.

Cat ignored him, finishing her point. "Proud."

Bash understood proud well enough. He'd been proud of being a huntsman. He was regularly proud of his siblings. Proud of what his family had achieved, too. Choosing to not attend a meeting where crucial information would be shared wasn't pride as much as stupidity.

Bash relaxed as they walked farther south, away from the pack. Fear wasn't stressing him out; he could have dealt with shifters back when he'd been a hunter. But he knew how volatile they were, and how much they hated vampires.

Like basically every other sup. Their longevity and power didn't endear them to anyone, to say nothing of their ability to rip open throats whenever they felt like it.

The vampires stopped at the edge of the border near the east train tracks.

Someone was there. Right at the edge. Observing the wards. Studying them.

Cat took one step forward. Bash opened his mouth to caution her, but, thinking better of it, decided to stay quiet. He didn't know whether their shield stopped sounds. Instead, he grabbed her hand.

Then he froze. He didn't expect the simple touch to feel so...noticeable.

She turned to him, eyes full of questions. Bash slowly shook his head, pulling his phone out. Shit. Did he have her number? He didn't think so.

He opened his notes app and wrote, *"He doesn't seem to know exactly where we are. Let's not clue him in."*

Cat didn't like it, but she acquiesced nonetheless, although she also grabbed her phone and started sending messages. To Levi, or Chloe, or any of the other vampires, Bash guessed. She wouldn't have thought to contact one person, though. So, Bash texted Jack to clue him in on the situation.

Mikar and Luke appeared next to them twenty-four seconds later. Levi and Chloe arrived shortly after, though his shirt was open and she wasn't wearing shoes. They were all silent as a tomb, eyes on the intruder.

He was rather plain. A man in his mid-thirties, perhaps, wearing a tracksuit and a sweater with the hood pulled low on his head. Because that wasn't conspicuous at all.

"A witch," Levi announced.

Oh, so they could talk.

"Don't they say wizard?" Chloe asked.

"Same difference. Witch, wizard, sorcerer, enchanter. That just means they're mortal and use magic," Cat replied.

"Right. Yeah, I knew that."

Bash didn't doubt Chloe had heard this before, but their brains were just so scattered after the change, it was hard to remember the simplest things, sometimes.

"And people who are sups for other reasons, like fangs or fur, but use magic anyway are mages?" Chloe wondered.

"Indeed. Although now may not be the right time to discuss terminology, sweet."

Levi sounded amused and rather patient, but his eyes, still set on the witch—wizard—were anything but. He looked like he might be wondering which one of his kitchen knives he should use to skin him alive.

"Did anyone contact Greer?"

"I'm here!"

They turned to find the witch running toward them, panting hard and holding her sides. If their attention hadn't been focused on the stranger, they would have heard or smelled her a lot sooner.

"Not all of us have superhuman speed, you know," she reminded them.

Mikar winked at her. "Holler next time. I'd carry you any day."

Bash was offended. Carry her? *Carry* her! What

happened to hunting people down and telling them he'd drink them dry if he caught them?

Apparently, that treatment was reserved for him. Or for vampires, in any case.

"All right, what have we here?" she asked as she reached them.

"You tell me," Levi replied, teeth grinding.

Seeing him defer to her was...unsettling.

Bash had always noticed something strange about Greer's position. She was accepted among the vampires, be they ancient or youth, and she'd also been invited to a conclave, unlike any other witch in the territory. Blair and Gwen—Chloe's friends—hadn't even walked on the hill more than once.

But that difference only now really hit him. She was treated like someone who truly mattered. Someone Levi trusted and relied on, like the slayers or Alexius. Which was more than what Bash could say. At best, he was a child they had to babysit.

"A dude. An ugly dude."

"Oh, shush!" Chloe said. "That's very superficial of you."

Greer shrugged, unapologetic. "I live around *GQ* model types. That dude is boring. Just saying it like it is."

"We don't care about whether you find the man attractive, Vespian. Is he a threat?"

"No."

"Yes."

The two replies had come at once, equally confident. Greer said no. Catherine disagreed.

The Whisper

Cat would have lied if she'd said she recognized the man at the border of Oldcrest; she'd never seen him. And if she had, she wouldn't have paid attention to him. He was one of thousands, a simple foot soldier of no consequence. But though she didn't know him, she could identify his energy easily enough.

"This place is sealed tight," Greer said. "It's held for over a thousand years against any intruder who hasn't been invited. There's no way this guy can get in."

Cat hated this. She'd planned to talk to Levi, but right now, it looked like she'd deliberately kept crucial information from them.

Which, admittedly, was exactly what she'd been doing. But only because she hadn't realized that knowledge was relevant until recently.

"Maybe," Cat said. "Maybe not. Well, it might be easier to just try it rather than explaining. Greer, how are your shields?"

Greer grinned, somewhat cockily. "All right," she replied. Meaning, awesome, obviously.

"Okay, can you build one around you? As strong as you can make it."

The witch nodded, then tightened her hands into fists, calling her energy.

Cat had seen mages and witches at work, but never had she felt the air burst around her with quite so much force as the light gray mist that gathered around Greer, followed by a darker energy, black as night. It formed a perfect sphere and then disappeared.

But she could still feel it.

Magic generally came in colors. Calling one specific energy brought forward particles with a shape and tone. Only the strongest creatures could render magic imperceptible.

Come to think of it, Cat had never seen Greer practice any magic until today. And now, she was sure she never wanted to see it again. Greer was known as a gifted potion master, not a spell caster. Now Cat understood: the witch was studying what she hadn't already mastered.

The woman was terrifying.

Cat tried not to feel self-conscious as she called to her storm again, drawing it to her. Unlike yesterday, she didn't attempt to summon all of the lightning she could withstand. Just a small taste. But usually, that was enough. Cat wasn't a strong mage. The smallest effort zapped her energy.

Today, she found the summoning a little bit easier. Maybe practice did make perfect after all.

She gathered the energy in her palms and threw it right at the witch. A bright white blast flashed from her palm to Greer, and hit the shield for a fraction of a second. Just a fleeting instant.

Her bolt zapped the shield, cracking the wards open on impact. Black and white particles fell to the ground around a shocked, open-mouthed Greer.

The other vampires were silent, and she could feel all eyes on her. Some curious, others frightened. Most, suspicious. She tried to not let it get to her.

"I'm not a particularly powerful mage in my family," she told them. "But my brother could potentially destroy the shields around Oldcrest. So could my aunt, and some others. This guy"—she pointed to the witch beyond the shield—"is a weather mage, like your friend Gwen. Only right now, he's concentrating on the storm. He's testing to see if it could destroy the wards around Oldcrest. In a few minutes, he'll figure out that he can fracture the defenses just a little bit. And he'll report that to my aunt, which is all she needs to know if she's planning on ordering an attack."

"And is she?" Levi asked. "Planning an attack."

Cat looked down at her toes. "I don't know."

She heard Mikar snort. "I *don't*," she insisted. "If you think for one minute Drusilla lets me in on her council, you have no idea who my aunt is."

"I think the most pressing matter is what we do with this," Chloe said, eyes still on the mage.

Levi thought for a moment.

"If he never shows up, someone else will be sent in his place. I say we need a compelling voice to convince him of what he should say when he returns to his masters, don't you think?"

Cat winced. She knew Chloe didn't like her whispering. The ability to control someone else's actions was a gift most would kill for, but the young vampire was too sweet and honest to like it.

But she nodded before stepping forward, leaving the safety of their territory.

Cat had to admit she was rather surprised that Levi allowed it. That he let her put herself in danger. Most dominant ancients would have balked against it and attempted to coddle her because of her youth. Instead, he gave her room to grow, to learn who she was.

What she was.

"Hello there," she said sweetly, and though she was facing Chloe's back, Cat imagined her friend was smiling. "Are you lost? I could show you the way."

The witch never had a chance.

Old Blood

"I suppose we'd better not delay this conversation any longer," Levi told Cat, who concurred. "Luke, cover the rest of her shift."

The assistant nodded.

"If Chloe is staying on the hill for the rest of the night, I'll cover the boy's shift."

Bash might have taken offense at being called a boy if it hadn't come from a creature quite as old and intimidating as Mikar. Besides, he had to admit he would have hated to finish his shift and miss what Catherine had to say.

Shit. He still had a hard time believing his eyes. To him, magic had always been logical. He'd studied it, and could understand the basics as well as any huntsman could. But there had been no logic to what he'd just seen. No rule or law. Only power. Infinite power.

They walked up the hill in silence, slowly, to accommodate Greer's pace. Levi led the way with

Chloe, and Catherine and the witch followed close behind while Bash brought up the rear.

Greer stopped in front of the Beaufort house, watching the damage Catherine had caused the previous night. She looked at the storm mage.

"Damn, woman."

Catherine shrugged. "I couldn't have taken on Anika in hand-to-hand combat on my best day. Drunk, I had no choice. So, magic. I don't think she expected that from me. If she heard details about me from my family, they would have told her I'm weak."

Bash snorted. What he'd witnessed the previous night and seen just now against Greer's shields, along with everything he'd seen from her since they met, said raw strength. Control like he could only dream of.

In his mind, vampires like him were monsters. Trying to reconcile himself with what he was now was nigh on impossible when every glance in the mirror, every breath he took, every unguarded thought reminded him of his desire for fresh blood.

He'd never hurt anyone. Even as a feral, thanks to his friends drugging and chaining him. He had crossed no lines, the rational part of him acknowledged that. He'd come close with Maddy, but Catherine had saved him. He was doing his best. Would a monster *try* that hard? Probably not.

But ridding himself of his beliefs, of the knowledge he'd taken for granted his whole life, was no small feat. Telling himself he was anything other than a freak had implications he wasn't sure he was ready to face.

Because if a bloodsucker desiring blood—and trying to hunt a poor wounded girl—wasn't evil, then who was?

Catherine was no different. She'd either been told or convinced herself that she was weak. And she wasn't ready to hear otherwise.

An ocean existed between facts and beliefs. And to cross it, they had to voluntarily take the jump.

When they reached the mansion, Levi headed up the grand staircase. Bash had never gone upstairs until today. Actually, he'd barely spent any time outside of the study where he'd been turned. Following the master of the house, they climbed two flights of stairs and reached a floor that didn't even seem to be part of the same house.

It looked...simple. Wooden flooring, cream walls with modern paintings—a superhero in flight to the right, a fairy in psychedelic tones on the left. The space was entirely open, with an alcove separating the large bedroom from the study-library area, music corner with instruments, and a large elevated platform with marble flooring and a sauna.

The height of modern comfort and minimalistic design. White furniture, nice beige rugs.

Levi removed his suit jacket and hung it on a hook at the entrance of his living space.

"Excuse the mess," he said.

The bed was unmade, and a couple of mugs sat on the coffee table, but the room didn't look messy as much as lived in.

"You should see Catherine's room," Bash replied.

That earned him a punch on the shoulder. He laughed as the vamp glared at him.

"Take a seat. Tea, coffee, wine, brandy, rum, vodka?"

"Sounds like an epic cocktail. Can you mix it all?" Chloe asked.

Everyone grimaced, none more than Catherine. "After yesterday, I've had a lifetime's worth of cocktails, thank you."

"Ah! Anika mixed you some magic, did she?" Levi asked, heading to his wooden bar between the bed and study. "Shame it was addled. She's quite a good bartender."

"It tasted lovely, but I'll still pass."

Levi chuckled. "Understandable. What can I get you?"

Catherine and Chloe opted for wine, and when Bash replied "anything," Levi made him his own drink of choice: a rum and Coke. They moved to the comfortable light brown sofa and armchair suite. Levi picked a loveseat, and Chloe hopped on his lap as though it was the most natural thing in the world.

They truly seemed to fit together effortlessly, like two halves of the same coin.

"I knew about the storms," Levi said, starting the conversation.

Catherine's eyes widened. "You did?"

He shrugged. "Your family and the rest of us may have grown suspicious and withdrawn to our own lands, but we were young once. And arrogant. Ariadne turned Drusilla somewhere around the start of the third century, if I'm not mistaken. I was one of Ariadne's slayers at the time, so I was there when she found a talented young air mage."

"The goddess has slayers?" Chloe seemed surprised.

Bash wasn't. He knew Ariadne kept four talented subordinates close to her at all times. Always four.

The huntsmen had hundreds of books about Ariadne, because while she was quiet these days, if she ever decided to cause havoc, she'd be one of the greatest threats Earth had ever faced. Her name was always said with a mixture of fear and respect, in that order. They hoped she'd never be an enemy. But they were prepared.

"Indeed. It's my understanding that her husband used to also keep four knights. She kept up the habit. In any case, Drusilla was talented but arrogant. These things often go hand in hand. Drusilla spent her first century challenging us—Jeremy Beaufort, Renee Rosedean, Tristan Helsing, and me—to show that she was better than us. She was under the misconception that if she won against us, Ariadne would pick her as a slayer. Eventually, she did win against Tristan, killing him in single combat. Instead of promoting her, Ariadne beat the crap out of her and told her to get out of Greece."

Bash's respect for the goddess went up a notch.

"No wonder Alexius doesn't like me," Catherine said. "My ancestor killed one of his."

Levi shook his head. "Oh, Alexius never knew Tristan. He was his...great uncle? I'm not certain. If Alex dislikes you, it's because he's...well, Alex."

No one asked him to elaborate. They weren't here to solve the mystery that was Alexius Helsing. Fortunately.

"She threw everything she had at us, and she could destroy any shield, any physical barrier. But she relied on her magic too much, and was weaker in hand-to-hand combat. Besides, calling her elements took time. It was easy enough to knock her down while she concentrated. That's why I seldom resort to magic myself," Levi explained. "I'm sure she's grown stronger with time." He shrugged, self-deprecating. "But then again, so have we all. Still, I'd wager she's stronger, and faster."

Why did he sound so damn matter-of-fact, relaxed even?

"So what do we do?" Chloe asked him.

Levi was staring at Catherine too intensely for Bash's liking.

"A few things can stop Stormhale magic, right, Cat?"

He knew the answer, that much was clear. He was testing Catherine, seeing if she was prepared to turn her back on her clan. Her family.

She nodded.

"Yes. Another Stormhale, for one. We're not allowed to fight each other with our lightning. If two powerful mages from my family truly attacked each other, the blast would burn everything and everyone in the vicinity to ashes."

"Indeed. And what else?"

She bit her lip, frowning a little. "Water. We're immune to most air magic, and lightning can't hurt us. But if we're in water..."

She didn't finish her sentence, gasping as she understood Levi's point at the same time as Bash.

"You could electrocute them all," Bash guessed. "If they turn up at the gates, you could flood them when they call their magic."

Levi smiled. "The so-called lake behind the hill is

no natural pool. It's a canal I carved. Not without reason. It's a dangerous tool, because I'd risk hurting our side, too, but we're not defenseless. However, with the Beauforts, all their mages, and who knows how many slayers, Drusilla could potentially take Oldcrest."

Shit.

"So, I assume we have a plan." At least, Bash hoped so.

"Indeed. We make alliances of our own. We have everything we need right here, but we're still missing trust. While the wolves stick to their borders and the vampires glare at the witches, the huntsmen stay among themselves. While we can't tell who might be working for the Stormhales, for the Beauforts, for the queen, it's unlikely that we can fight as one. I will need you to cross those bridges. All three of you, along with everyone else."

"I'm game." Chloe's quick agreement was unsurprising.

Catherine and Bash nodded.

Bash thought he knew what his mission would be. Talk to Jack. Speak to the huntsmen about opening up to the bloodsuckers.

"Good. Bash, I want you to start a self-defense class. In your spare time, you will train whoever wants to sign up. Level: beginners. Chloe, you will move from the dorm and take up residence where you belong." She opened her mouth to protest against moving in with him, no doubt, but Levi ended his sentence, surprising them all, with, "In Skyhall."

The house at the very top of the hill that Eirik

had built, the house her ancestors had inhabited until they were slaughtered.

"Why? That makes no sense. How would that help at all?"

"The world is changing, *ma belle*. It changed when you were turned. There hasn't been order on this hill since the days of the Eirikrsons. We have dozens of queens, ten kings. The person who plays at being queen on her island never had a chance. Our world has barely acknowledged her until today. But now, because you and Tom changed, whether we like it or not, Night Hill is once again seen as the seat of power to our kind. We are the true immortal power in this world. And there will be challenges. From the Stormhales, from the queen, from the Drakes, the Helsings, the Beauforts, the Rosedeans, and just about everyone who believes they can take our seat. My family, perhaps. Making our allies believe they stand a chance will take everything we have. They won't fight for a dream. But they might fight for a place in an empire. Our homes are kingdoms. The seats of power for each of our houses. The world sees them that way, so it's time we do, too. Skyhall is no house. It's a throne."

"You're saying they will see more of a reason to fight if we reinstate the order. If I march into Skyhall and act like I own it."

"You do own it. If our students are afraid, they'll look to the Hill. Its strongest holdfast cannot remain empty."

Chloe remained silent, and Levi moved on to Catherine. "As for you—"

She braced herself, ready for the worst.

"You will start an afternoon tea club in your house on the hill."

Bash thought about their orders. "You're trying to make us seem less threatening."

"We'll always be a threat to our enemies. I'm trying to show our potential friends who we are underneath the violence and bloodthirst. It's time to open this hill. We're enough, if we're together. This is just the first step to uniting Oldcrest."

Bash could tell Chloe was trying to work out a way to protest, but Levi turned to them. "You had something to say, Cat."

She nodded. "I think you may not know the recent developments among my family."

Levi inclined his head. "You're probably right."

"My mother is a Stormhale, and she married one of the family slayers thirty years ago. I'm their first child; my little sister is the second. But my brother..." Catherine knotted her hands on her lap.

She hated speaking about her siblings.

"My *half*-brother isn't like Drusilla. He doesn't share her limits. He might be young, but he's...something else. If Drusilla gets him to fight us, he'd burn you all to a crisp before you can even think to use whatever magic you may possess."

Levi lifted one brow.

"Every mage needs time."

"Yes. But my brother's father was a scion. You may need a minute. Seth will be ready in a fraction of a second."

Levi groaned. "I hate nephilim." He turned to Bash. "Call Jack."

Catherine winced. "This is not common knowl

edge. If the information gets out, my family will know it came from me."

"Jack can keep a secret," Chloe promised.

"Besides, we need him to know what to expect. If he hears this now, he might get his shit together and prepare accordingly."

Bash wasn't fond of the turn in the conversation. "Jack is always prepared for a fight."

"Yes, yes." Levi was dismissive. "He gets his friends to run around the territory and attends whatever class he's supposed to take. But he does nothing to better *himself*. And right now, we need Jack Hunter."

He wanted to defend his friend, but come to think of it, had Bash ever seen Jack exert himself? He ran alongside them without breaking a sweat and while wearing suits. When he sparred with his cousin, he didn't even pant.

Bash knew what Jack was—every huntsman did. The kid of their High Guard and a minor god. The blood of a huntsman mixed with that of a true immortal.

What were his limits?

It irked Bash that Levi seemed to know more than he did about his best friend.

He nodded and pulled out his phone, sending a quick text.

We need to talk.

Wings and Fury

C at didn't know why she was tagging along with Bash, but he hadn't protested, so she followed him down the west flank of the hill toward the lake.

They found the gate closed. Bash tried to open it, and winced.

"Shit. The bloody thing shocked me. Magic shields."

Cat chuckled. "Here, let me."

She stepped forward and opened it, ignoring his protests. The handle gave in when she tugged it down.

"Stormhale, remember? The hill is warded against outsiders."

Bash rolled his eyes, muttering something probably true about nepotism.

They spotted Jack by the lakeside as soon as they turned down the path. He was standing in front of the lake, practicing the violin. Although he hit a few wrong notes, the man played with feeling and skill. A rendition of a pop song Cat couldn't remember. It had never sounded quite so good.

He finished the song and turned to greet them.

"I didn't know you played," Sebastian said.

Jack shrugged. "I used to as a kid. I stopped after moving here. I didn't have an instrument."

"You could have bought one," Catherine pointed out.

"I didn't have the time," Jack amended. "Besides, I mostly played for my mother. No one here would care to listen to an average violinist. But I digress. Your text said you had to speak to me urgently."

Bash nodded. "Yeah. Something Levi said."

Cat saw Jack's back stiffen and his eyes narrow.

"I know what the Leviathan wants of me," he replied. "Just because he embraces being a monster doesn't mean the rest of us have to. Is that all?"

"There have been developments. Levi thinks we may need your monster. Whatever that is."

Sebastian glanced at Cat, and she could tell he wished she weren't there.

"Look, I get it. I feel like that. Like I'm out of control. Like these new...gifts of mine make me a monster, because it feels unnatural. But it's who I am now. And whatever you are, you were born that way."

"You have no clue what you're talking about. You, Tris, even that damn sucker. You're *human*. Red blood runs in your veins. You may have been turned, infected, changed, but you're part of this world, made to exist on Earth."

"And you're not?" Sebastian snorted. "Your mom is a hunter, descended from the very first huntsman trained by Eirikr. The Venaris were the second. Whatever I am, we *are* brothers. The blood in our veins is the same. Or it was."

It happened so fast that Cat couldn't have stopped it even if she'd been prepared. One moment they were all standing close together, and the next, she and Bash were both firmly pinned to the ground, her chest crushed under heavy weight. Cat was too shocked to even try to break free.

Two sets of humongous wings with pure white feathers had burst out of his back, destroying his suit in the process and pushing them down on their asses. Cat didn't even think Jack had done it on purpose.

Jack's wings moved, somewhat reluctantly, to extend at his sides. And now that he'd revealed his true form, his eyes were dark as night, hollow.

He tucked the wings behind him, and they slowly crawled back inside his skin. The glint in his eyes disappeared. Jack turned around. Four ugly scars ran from his neck to the bottom of his shoulder blades.

"Tell me we're the same now."

Sebastian was speechless.

"Even among the gods themselves," Jack said, "my kind is known to be wild. The Skylars, we're called. Most of the Enlightened avoid them. The wings have a will of their own. Making them move consciously takes more strength than anything I've ever done. There's an actual beast inside. It doesn't recognize you, or my cousin, or my own mother as an ally. If I let them, the wings would impale anyone who gets too close to me in my sleep. Every day, that thing tries to win, tries to take control of me. There's a Mr. Hyde crawling inside me. You're no monster, Bash. Not compared to me."

Well, that was quite enough of that.

Catherine pushed to a crouch and lunged at the man, feigning to aim for his chest but jumping down to trip him before shoving her heel to his throat.

"What is it with huntsmen and their poor footwork?" she mused, before redirecting her attention to the man under her foot. "First things first. You do not touch me, or any other lady, without her express invitation. Tell *that* to your damn wings. Shove me, and you'll get kicked sevenfold. Second thing: enough with the self-pity. You're pathetic. The emo thing has a sixteen-year-old expiration date. Get your damn shit together, huntsman. Because if you don't, your friends are screwed."

"My friends—" he croaked.

She lifted her heel just high enough for him to speak.

"My friends do just fine. I train them to the best of my ability."

"But no one trains you. Clearly," she added, waving toward his body, still on the ground. "If I can take you, you wouldn't last a minute against Seth."

"Wait, who's Seth?"

Cat finally moved her heel away.

"My brother. Another one of *you*. Half scion, or whatever you call yourselves these days. We may be able to deal with my family, with the Beauforts, and maybe even with the queen, but not one of us can take my brother. And Levi thought you might be able to." She grimaced. "I doubt it."

Jack leaped to his feet.

"What sort of threat are we talking about?"

"A storm," she replied.

Jack tilted his head. "Storms have no effect on me. No air magic does."

No wonder Levi had wanted to rope him in against Seth.

"Good. But Seth will still kick your ass. You're out of shape."

"I let you knock me over, woman."

She snorted. "Right. Keep telling yourself that."

❦

"MY DARLING BOY! WE DIDN'T EXPECT YOU FOR some time."

Seth smiled pleasantly at the family matriarch, as he always did. It wouldn't do to bare his teeth in front of a predator such as her.

"You call, I answer, Aunt Drusilla."

She laughed and opened her arms to cage him in.

Many believed that Seth Stormhale's greatest power was over the storms. He disagreed. His true gift was his uncanny ability to see through bullshit.

Drusilla was so full of it.

She'd told him to come the first week of July. He knew that meant she wanted him then and not one minute sooner.

After checking with his cousins scattered around the world, Seth's suspicions were confirmed. Everyone had been recalled. Which meant one thing.

The clan was preparing for war.

He wasn't against it. He'd expected such a call since the moment the world had heard about her.

Chloe Eirikrson. A relic from an old world the vampires had tried to bury. And failed.

Seth was easily bored, and he had to admit the situation was incredibly *interesting*.

"You must be tired from your journey. I'll have your quarters prepared at once."

"No need to rush the staff, Aunt Dru, it's my fault for failing to warn you of my arrival. I'll stay with Claudia until my rooms are set up."

He'd intended to speak to his sister in any case. She might be young, but she had eyes and ears that worked just as well as any other spy's.

"I'm afraid Claudia's away at the moment, but her rooms should be empty if you want to rest."

Away? That made little sense. At eighteen, the girl was rarely permitted outside of Stormhall, to Seth's knowledge. The Stormhales were protective of their youth.

"Where is she?"

Drusilla said some words, gave explanations. All Seth heard was more bullshit.

He made up an excuse and walked through the familiar palazzo until he'd reached his little sisters' apartments. Catharina used to have the right side and Claudia the left, but now that the elder of the two was in Scotland, his youngest sibling had claimed the entire floor. It was pristine. Not one cushion out of place.

"Cendric."

The window flew open in less than ten seconds. A large man, fast as a shadow, appeared. Cendric was the oldest and strongest among the Stormhale guards and slayers. The true leader of their forces.

The seventy-year-old vampire took one step forward before dropping to his knees.

"My lord."

He had many questions. But first things first.

"My sister. Report."

Underneath It All

Bash couldn't stop smiling as they headed back to the dorms. He didn't think he'd ever seen anyone get the better of Jack that way.

"What?" Catherine snapped.

He might have been staring for too long.

"I'm just amazed by the extent of your apathy. I didn't think it was possible for anyone to hear a sad story and react with so little compassion. Do you kick puppies, too?"

Catherine rolled her eyes. "Your friend didn't need compassion. He's feeling sorry enough for himself. He needed a reality check."

"Like me," Bash added.

She shrugged. "Think what you will. I can show compassion. To those whose misery isn't of their own making."

Fast as they were, they reached the doors in no time. Bash found that he didn't want to say goodbye quite yet. Even though he had a paper to write, and apparently, a self-defense class to prepare for, he liked Catherine's company.

"Shall we play a game?" He immediately regretted the question.

She didn't look like the type of person who enjoyed wasting her time like that.

"What sort of a game?"

He shrugged. "A videogame. There are some in the common room. Not sure which. Or chess, if you prefer. You'd definitely have a better chance of winning at that, I'd wager."

Catherine shrugged. "Sure thing. Let's try a video game."

※

THE WOMAN WAS SERIOUSLY ANNOYING. WAS THERE anything she didn't excel at?

"Again," he growled, pressing the button to start a new challenge.

He hadn't played the racing track in a while, but after a single race, where he'd happily smashed her by a full minute, Catherine had memorized all commands. She pulled moves he'd never seen in his life, shoving her car at just the right angle to hit a code up in the air and then reappearing a mile up the road.

"What the *hell* was that?"

"No one likes a sore loser."

"No one likes a perfect Barbie robot, damn you!"

She snorted. "As far as insults go, I'm sure you could do better."

Losing again, although it had been his best time,

he threw the remote control across the sofa. Time to admit defeat and lick his wounds.

Bash glared at Catherine.

"Admit it. You played that game before."

She grinned. "Only for fifteen years or so."

Bash laughed, half relieved, because maybe she was human after all, and half incredulous. She really didn't strike him as the sort of woman who could let her hair down and chill. But then again, he'd seen her room. And he knew she loved to pause and watch all sorts of creatures.

There were two Catherines, he realized. The cold, unfeeling front she showed to the world, and the other one. Softer. Not kinder, exactly, but certainly more real. He wondered how many people got to see her. He wondered how many people got to *touch* her.

But he couldn't.

"You can be kind of fun, Stormhale. When you want to."

She snorted. "That's a far leap from hating me a week ago."

He'd said that, hadn't he? "Fine. Maybe I don't hate you. It's just fucking frustrating how easily you seem to waltz through life. Perfect at everything. Being a lady, a vampire, a goddamn videogame player."

Catherine took a swig of beer. "Maybe we aren't as different as I first thought. I watch you struggle with something that seems so simple to me, and I find it frustrating as hell, too, you know. The composure? That's normally easy to me. Effortless. I only got where you came from after tasting true hunger. Before, I couldn't even comprehend it clearly. But just because I don't suffer from thirst like you doesn't mean I don't have problems."

He wasn't sure he would have believed that earlier, but after the last few days, he got it. She had one issue: her last name. And everything and everyone who went with it.

Rather than voicing his guess, he asked, "What kind of problems?"

She seemed startled by his curiosity.

"Well, you shove your nose in my business and tell me what to do. I should do the same. Even out in the field."

She rolled her eyes. "All right. So, my problem is my siblings."

He hadn't expected that.

"You have two, right?"

Catherine nodded. "Yes, Seth and Claudia. Our extended family is full of bullshit and complication, but the three of us...we have fun, you know? Sure, I bicker with Claudia. All the time. She sneaks into my closet and steals my shoes. Then she spars with them and brings them back unpolished."

She was grinning from ear to ear, proving she didn't really mind. Bash gasped dramatically. "No!"

"I didn't even tell you the state my favorite suede boots were in after she took them on a damn hunt. And Seth is...a lot. Megalomaniacal as hell. He doesn't even believe he can lose or be wrong. The annoying thing is, he's generally right."

Catherine Stormhale had never looked quite so human. Relatable. Bash looked away; if he didn't, he might end up pulling her to him. Touching her. Kissing her.

She'd been clear. No more kissing. He wasn't one to ignore a woman's wishes.

But trying to convince her to change her mind had never been quite so tempting.

"So what's the issue?"

She sighed. "There's a war coming, and we aren't on the same side."

Oh. Yeah, that.

"If it came down to stopping my uncles and aunts from entering Oldcrest, I wouldn't think twice. I'd fight them." A laugh escaped her delicious lips. "I might even enjoy it, in some cases. But Claudia or Seth..."

"No one is asking you to fight your brother or sister."

She nodded. "I know. But that's what it comes down to, even if I don't face them directly. A line has been drawn between our clan and Oldcrest. They're with Stormhall, and I'm here."

Bash tried to imagine fighting against Emilia and Paul, but the notion was inconceivable. Whatever line there was, he'd cross it and drag them both along by his side.

"Do they have to be?" he asked her. "On the other side. Have you asked them what they think?"

He regretted his question. It was too simple. Of course she'd thought of that.

"I can't. I can't contact them on my family's network. You don't know what it's like in Stormhall. There are servants everywhere, reporting on our every move. Our emails are watched, too."

Bash said, "Sure. Too bad you don't have a witch

friend or two who could help you send some secret correspondence, right?"

Catherine blinked. She clearly hadn't considered that.

Then she bit her lips. "It'd be dangerous. Claudia could go straight to Drusilla. She could be ordered to spy for her, or worse."

"It comes down to how much you trust your siblings."

Silence stretched between them. Her forehead wrinkled as she considered her options.

Then, she said, "That was...strangely enlightening. I should chat with you more often."

Bash laughed. "Yeah, you should." He didn't want her to go, so out of curiosity, he added, "What about your parents?"

For some reason, he expected her face to turn somber, but instead, she smiled again.

"They're irrelevant. When it comes to fighting and sides and wars, anyway. My mom was always a free spirit. A vampire hippie, if you would."

Bash tried to imagine that. A Catherine with flowers in her hair, dancing barefoot. He laughed his ass off. "I would love to meet her."

"No, you would not," she replied firmly. "Anyway, she was always a great disappointment to the part of my family who's after power—Aunt Drusilla, her own parents, basically everyone. Fortunately, she was the youngest of five children, all four more useful than she, so they mostly left her alone. Josephine—that's her name—is incredibly beautiful. The prettiest among us, I'd say. Drusilla made her have a fling with a male scion once. Seth's father. Then, when that ended, Aunt Drusilla brought Seth to Stormhall and left her alone. She has a palazzo in Venice, away from Stormhall. My mom travels the world and has as much fun as she can muster. She had a bodyguard following her around, of course. And thirty years ago, she married him. They still travel all the time."

Bash wasn't sure he liked Josephine anymore. "What about you and Claudia?"

"We were also sent to Stormhall when we were old enough."

"How old?" There was an edge to his tone.

"Five. That's when our training starts."

His jaw was set. Huntsman training didn't start much later, but they weren't plucked from their parents' house.

"Don't pity me. It was all right."

But it wasn't. He could see in her eyes that it wasn't. Things had happened to her during her training. Things that explained why she was so closed off, so guarded. He could tell, just as he could tell she wouldn't discuss it with him.

"All right. I won't pity you. But I may just kiss you, though."

He wasn't a saint, for heaven's sake.

As no protest crossed her lips, Bash drew close to her and dropped his mouth to hers, tasting her sweetness again.

There it was. The peace, the fire, the desire he'd missed for two fucking weeks. He felt like he was breathing again after drowning. He felt alive.

He was just about to let go, not wanting to freak

her out again, when Catherine pulled away and got to her feet. She turned around slowly and looked over her shoulder.

"Well, what are you waiting for?" she asked, before leading the way to her room.

Wordless

C at had a code. A rule about the people around her. Back in Stormhall or here, she just didn't shit where she slept. It was common sense. The problem was that after sex, men expected more sex, or a clear break-up speech. Cat wasn't against repeating good sex, of course, but good sex was hard to come by. Most of the time, it was either boring or average. She was done after one night. Breaking up with a guy who lived just one floor below her was messy. A mess she couldn't afford.

But she wanted him. Simple. So she brought him upstairs and resumed their embrace.

The moment his hands touched her thighs, all words got stuck in her throat. She gasped as Sebastian inched his fingers up the hem of her skirt while exploring her lips leisurely, as though he had all the time in the world.

She shifted on the sofa to straddle his lap, looking down at his face, her hands on either side of his neck. His eyes were bright red. Hungry. *Thirsty*. With so

183

much desire in his gaze, she would have expected him to rush, to pull his dick and stuff it right inside her. Instead, he kissed the line of her collarbone while caressing her thigh.

Cat opened the buttons of his light blue cotton shirt one by one, revealing every inch of his hard chest.

"This means nothing," she said, finally.

Sebastian chuckled against her shoulder, wordlessly biting the collar of her dress and pulling it down with his teeth.

She needed him to accept her terms. He had to agree it was just some no-strings-attached fun before it was too late.

"I mean—"

I mean it. That's what she was about to tell him. But his lips closed over the top of her breast, and he brushed down the strap of her bra, lowering the cup and wrapping his mouth around her nipple. Then, he sucked.

Words were overrated.

His tongue darted out, circling her sensitive flesh, until she was nothing but a spineless, moaning form curving into his touch. Cat whined when his mouth left her breast, but she was quick to shut up. Bash kissed down her stomach, hands on her hips, pulling her dress up. He flipped her around, laying her on her messy bed, and knelt at the edge, kissing her hipbone and then her inner thigh.

Then he laughed, looking up at her.

"Bunnies?"

Cat glanced down and almost died of embarrassment. Damn, she'd forgotten she was wearing white cotton panties with bunnies on them. She had fancy lace underwear, black or red silk, and also the occasional cute cotton shortie, but she didn't pay much attention to what she put on in the morning. Unless she actually planned on getting laid.

"A gentleman would have ignored that."

"Good thing I'm no gentleman. You know, Catherine, sometimes I think I might like you. I definitely like your mouth, and your breasts, and your ass." As he talked, the infuriating man edged around her panties, his fingers teasing her. She felt her insides contract, needing more, needing him to touch her right there. "But this underwear," Sebastian said, hooking his fingers at each side and pulling them down, "I actually love."

He slid them down her legs and gathered the panties in a fist before putting them in his pocket.

"You're not taking those."

"Stop me," he challenged, before diving face first at her pussy.

She might have tried, if her entire body hadn't frozen and then curved as she moaned. Fuck, he was good. *Great.* Sebastian's tongue was focusing on her clit, pushing it, licking it, while two fingers curved inside her. A trail of curses escaped Cat's lips. In Italian. Or maybe French. She couldn't tell. But she was shouting. Cat wasn't usually that vocal.

She brought her pillow to her mouth and bit down, self-conscious. It muffled her scream, but she couldn't stop fidgeting, trying to get closer and attempting to flee all at once.

"Oh, no, no, no. I don't think so." Sebastian emerged, but kept his fingers inside her, and replaced his mouth with his thumb, still toying with her. "The pillow goes. Or I stop."

If he stopped, she might die. And she'd definitely kill him.

With a groan, she threw the pillow down on the floor and winced, panting and doing her best to remain silent.

Sebastian moved up the bed, his right hand staying at the apex of her thighs, and returned to her breast— the left one this time.

"Scream for me, pretty girl."

His maddening fingers on her clit and inside her changed rhythm, pushing harder, and his mouth around her sensitive chest sucked and nibbled harder. Cat panted and moaned, writhing, needing air, until she crashed down the edge of a cliff she hadn't even seen coming.

Fuck. This wasn't supposed to be so good. She'd never come with a man touching her. Her wand and vibrators? Sure. But guys weren't supposed to actually know what to do with a female body. Especially guys his age. Sebastian must have had a great deal of practice, and she was grateful for his mastery in the art of sex. Grateful enough to crawl to him as soon as she was capable of moving and hook her fingers around the belt of his chinos.

"This needs to go," she told him, unzipping his pants.

He was quick to comply, removing his belt as she worked to free his hard cock from his black boxers.

"You don't need to—"

His sentence ended on a sharp hiss, because her mouth had taken the head of his cock, and her tongue was tracing its edges. She wasn't a master at sucking cocks, but after his performance, she definitely tried her best, taking her time. She licked the bottom from base to tip before taking the length down her throat, as far as she could go, and sucking. Her head went down, she sucked harder, breathing as she lifted it. Sebastian's hips thrust to meet her. He fisted her hair, and his nails scratched her scalp. She could tell he was trying to be gentle, but every time her mouth returned to the base of his cock, he thrust a little faster, tightened his fist harder. He grunted, and she couldn't recall ever feeling quite so powerful, like this hunter, this beast, was at her mercy. Right now, she could have demanded the moon and he would have asked whether she preferred a silver or golden bow on it.

"Shit, Catherine, I'm gonna come. You should stop..."

Stop? No fucking way? She blew him harder and faster, feeling his butt tighten under her hands, his thrusts become faster, shallower. He panted before tightening everywhere. Catherine sucked him right in her throat, immediately swallowing the salty, acidic cum without tasting it. No one needed that on their tongue.

Sebastian let go of her hair, bent forward, and laughed. "Shit, woman. They always say the crazy ones are better in bed."

"Oh, I'm crazy?"

He turned on his back and pulled her close. "Abso lutely. Crazy beautiful. Crazy good at head. And, in a minute, crazy good at taking cocks, too."

She snorted. "How presumptuous of you. What

makes you think I want to take your cock anywhere else?"

"Oh, I see the lady may need a little more convincing."

He climbed on top of her, arms either side of her face, his dick, already hard, right against her entrance. He rubbed himself against her, instantly awakening every part of her. Then Sebastian kissed her again. This time, it was demanding. No more patience and sweetness. He fucked her mouth with his tongue, and fucked her clit and pussy lips with his cock. He fucked her thighs too. She was dripping, moaning, her thoughts incoherent again.

"Tell me now how you don't want my cock, Catherine."

"Please!"

Fuck. She wasn't even sorry about begging. She *needed* him.

"Please what, crazy, beautiful Cat?" He stilled. "Do you want me to stop?"

Desperately, she yelled, "No, please! Please don't stop. I need you. I need you inside me now!"

He grinned and kissed the top of her head before entering her in one hard thrust, filling her so deep.

"Now," he said, tilting his hips forward as Cat clutched the sheets, mouth hanging open, "we may discuss what this means."

He punctuated his words with another deep thrust that made her feel him everywhere inside her.

Sebastian knelt again, lifting her hips so that he hit her at just the right spot, and swayed his hips. Cat brought her hands to her breasts, squeezing them.

"God."

"To me, this means I like you. And that I trust you enough to not plant a knife in my back as I come."

She would have replied, but she was too busy seeing stars, robbed of speech and vision, incapable of the slightest clear thought.

"And it means you like me."

His thumb was on her clit, pressing it, pinching it, and in that moment, she didn't like him at all.

"You may, of course, stop liking me, or stop *wanting* me. And I could potentially cease to like you. Lose my mind and stop desiring your tight, hot, perfect pussy. If either of those things do occur, we may end this arrangement any time. But for now, Catherine Stormhale..." He bent forward, left arm under her back, right at her shoulder blades, and pulled her up onto his hips. His next words were but a whisper on her neck. "I intend to convince you to let me take you again and again."

Status Quo

27

Catherine's body usually healed at record speed, but when she woke up, she still felt Sebastian. An ache deep inside her. He hadn't been kidding about the again and again bit. She woke up alone on a bed that smelled of him. And she only had three seconds to realize she didn't like it before her door opened to reveal him wearing nothing but boxers and holding a tray of food.

She laughed. "You walked the corridors half naked?"

He rolled his eyes, kicking the door closed. "I dare say everyone here has seen boxers. And I was famished. You're insatiable."

Cat chuckled again. "Yeah, right. It was all me."

"Glad that you're taking responsibility."

He put the tray down on her bed. Two plates of croissants, bacon, eggs, coffee, and blood on the side.

She could get used to this.

"What time is it?"

"Noon. I have class in an hour. Although, I'm not sure who that'll be with."

Ah, yes, Anika had taught one of his classes.

"Do you know what happened to her?" Cat asked. "Anika."

"Levi locked her up in his lab, under the Institute. He had cages made for our kind. He said he would have cut her head off if she weren't a Beaufort, but it isn't worth open war with her family. There'll be a judgment. Her family will send a defender."

Vampire trials were rare, particularly among the seven. Cat didn't think any had happened in her lifetime.

For someone as well known and prominent as Anika, the trial would be a grand affair. Each house would send a representative, and a well-known impartial judge would be appointed.

"What charges would she be accused of?" Cat wondered. "Sure, she betrayed Oldcrest, but that's not technically illegal."

"Poisoning you," Sebastian replied. "That should be enough to ban her from the country. That's all Levi wants right now."

Smart. Then, if and when she came back, she'd have a price on her head any vampire could claim.

"A trial is risky, though. If it's to be held here."

All those people would come through the border. Who knew where everyone's alliances lay?

"Levi says they'll hold it in London."

That made sense. He wouldn't risk Chloe's safety. Or anyone else's, for that matter.

They ate in silence. She was thinking about the trial, and the sex, and her family, and the sex again.

"What's your schedule like?" Sebastian asked.

"I don't have class until Business at three, but I figured I'd start my assignment. You know, set up the afternoon tea for this weekend." She rolled her eyes. "I'll design a pamphlet and get it printed in the Adairford shop. Then, I have Mr. Silver, a break, Varra this evening, and sentinel until six. Fridays are light for me."

Sebastian grinned. "Sounds like we might have a break at the same time. How about..."

"We're *not* going to exhaust ourselves before patrolling," she said.

He grinned. "I was going to suggest dinner, naughty girl. Get your head out of the gutter. The exhaustion comes after patrol."

"I probably can't make dinner," she replied, not bothering to deny the possibility of post-patrol exercise. "I'll be training Chloe."

"Fine. Saturday. Outside of here. We can have lunch in Edinburgh or whatever."

Cat wrinkled her nose. "Why go all the way there?"

"Because Adairford is pathetic and I want to take you on a decent date."

He did?

She froze, and blinked.

Catherine had never actually gone on a date.

"That's probably a terrible idea."

"I know, but we're still doing it. I'll make reservations and text you the time later."

He was taking charge, and she wasn't sure she disliked that, dammit. Cat was completely out of her depth. She blamed the many orgasms for her lack of wit and discernment. They'd short-circuited her brain or something.

"I don't know. There's a potential attack from my family, and the Beauforts, and that queen. It doesn't feel like the right time for a date."

"I was a huntsman. My parents were huntsmen too. There was always a crisis—a rogue, shifter, demon, vampire, or necromancer. A witch sacrificing babies somewhere. And yet every Tuesday night, they went out on a date, pretending the world wasn't on fire around them. Dad used to say it was their sanity day. All the anxiety, the anticipation, the hunt can consume our lives if we let it. So I say lunch, and sex, and chilling occasionally are all brilliant ideas."

Sebastian made a good case.

"I stopped living after being bitten. Stopped fighting. And I was miserable. If I am going to survive hundreds of years, I'd rather make it a fun ride."

"Carpe diem," she whispered.

"Way to summarize an eloquent speech with an overused idiom, Stormhale."

"Well, if the shoe fits." She polished off her plate and stretched out on her bed. "But fine. I'll free up tomorrow afternoon."

"Good girl." He leaned forward, pressing his lips on hers in an unexpected and gentle kiss that made her feel as unsettled as when he'd played her pussy with his tongue.

Damn him. What was he doing to her?

"I have to get changed. Catch you for patrol, pretty girl."

"I'm no girl, Sebastian."

"No? You didn't mind my calling you that yesterday. And for heaven's sake, my name is Bash."

"I like Sebastian," she replied stubbornly. "It suits you."

"Have you been talking to my sister? She's the only other person who persists on using my full name."

Cat laughed. "A woman of great taste. And you call me Catherine, anyway, so we're even. Now go get some clothes on. I have stuff to do."

And if he remained naked here, she wasn't going to do them. She devoured him with her eyes, appreciating every delightful muscle, the way his arms flexed as he walked away.

Come to think of it, her to-do list wasn't that full right now.

"Wait."

He turned back to her, one eyebrow raised. She flipped the bedsheet off her naked frame.

"Well, I do have a couple of hours to kill. No one said I had to start designing now."

Paper and Needles

CHAPTER
28

I t so happened that Chloe didn't want to spar tonight. Cat received a raven right after her business lesson.

"Hey! I have a race with Tris and the others tonight. Sparring tomorrow?"

Cat groaned, scribbling on the other side of the note before sending the bird right back.

"Sure, in the evening. I'll be out during the day."

She was annoyed at herself for turning down dinner with Sebastian tonight.

By the time Cat reached Adairford, the bird was back.

"You wanna meet us for drinks at the Snuggy Snot after? We should be done by eight."

Cat sent a quick yes, and after debating the issue, asked the bird, "Can your master send another message for me?"

The raven chirped something that sounded like an agreement.

"Good. To Bash—Sebastian Venari."

She pulled out a piece of paper and wrote, "*Snuggy Snot, 8—A Pretty Girl*."

Cat entered the printer's shop in town feeling quite greedy.

There were only a few businesses in Adairford, selling the kind of stuff college students stuck so far from civilization would find necessary. A pub—most of them were of age, after all, although a few geniuses in their teens had entered the Institute a time or two. A sports apparel store, essential for their intense training. A few clothing stores, a pharmacy, an apothecary that sold most of the ingredients needed for the crafting of spells, and, of course, a printer. Personal home printers worked well enough for notes and exercises, but most people liked to make their reports pretty.

In her six months here, Cat had become a regular. She liked binding her documents and using nice, heavy-grained paper.

"Oh, hello there!"

"Mrs. Lowery. I hope I didn't catch you at an inconvenient time."

The owner of Thin Tree was a plump sixty-year-old with long white hair. The store looked a lot like a cozy living room, with a foyer and an armchair close to the fireplace where she liked to knit.

Mrs. Lowery's sister taught spells to post-grads. She also liked to knit, but her knitting involved needles crossing in mid-air in the corner of the classroom while she taught. Cat had heard a rumor that in the winter, the woman distributed scarves, gloves, and sweaters to everyone in town.

"Oh, shush. You could never disturb me. Let me just get that knot right, and then I'll be with you shortly. You want to pick your binding while I work? I got new colors in."

"Oh, I'm not here to print a lesson. Don't mind me, I'll just look at your displays for a minute."

She paged through the printer's catalogue and chose a thick pink paper. Cat pulled out her computer and adapted the design she'd been working on to fit the paper's circular shape.

She'd kept things simple: the doodle of a teapot and a cup in one corner, then a short, "You're convivially invited for afternoon tea at Number Three, Night Hill, on Sunday at four. RSVP by Friday."

She'd signed the invitation by hand to make it look a little more personal. Having the tea this Sunday didn't leave much notice, but the term ended tomorrow. They had a six-week summer break after that. Cat, always the overachiever, wanted to get the ball rolling before most of Oldcrest returned home for the summer.

"Oh! Afternoon tea. And on the hill, too. How delightful, dear. In my day, I would have squealed for something quite as exciting."

"You studied here?" Cat asked, somewhat surprised.

The older woman laughed. "No, I think not. I was never the studious one. But I was born here. My mother used to own this shop, and her father, and his mother before that, back since the days when we would be copying the speeches the lords of the hill gave us. I went away for high school, and then came right back. There's something about this place. It's impossible to leave. The rest of the world feels wild. And dirty."

Cat understood what she meant. The air was clear here—they barely used cars, and no factories were near.

Oldcrest might have been a little quiet if not for the company of many young sups. And hot teachers. And the occasional attack. Plus the underlying threats from many sides.

Come to think of it, Oldcrest wasn't quiet at all.

"But I've never been on the hill. Not once. I would have been so very excited if this had happened back when I was young."

"Well, you should join us, then. When do you think the invites will be ready?"

"It depends on how many you would like."

Cat thought for a moment. The house wasn't as grand as Levi's home, but a few of the rooms were large enough to fit four dozen people. The weather was kind this time of the year, and if she set up a tent in the garden, she could house the entire Institute, the staff, all of Adairford, and even the shifters in the Wolvswoods. Which wasn't saying much. Overall, perhaps five hundred people lived here. Less than three hundred students, a hundred staff, two dozen teachers...

She doubted everyone would take the invitation, but she could plan for a big event and scale down as needed.

"Five hundred, if you would."

"Oh my! Well, I'll get started right now. They will be ready by morning, latest. I could rush them if you needed me to..."

"Morning is soon enough."

She paid for the invitations, and added a generous tip, before heading back to the dorm. She had a couple of hours until she needed to head over to the pub. Maybe she should take a nice bubble bath.

Cat opened the door to the dorm's right wing and found herself face to face with Jack.

"I was waiting for you," he said.

Cat stiffened. She didn't know what this was about, but she didn't like it.

"What for?"

He stuffed his hands into the pockets of his suit and shrugged.

"You were right. I don't train myself. Because no one I've ever been sent to fight is a challenge. I don't need to. I *didn't* need to."

Cat waited for him to get to the point.

"If your brother comes here to attack us, I'll have to do something about it. I'd rather not die in the process."

"Not dying is always a good thing. What do you want from me?"

The huntsman grinned.

"Levi sent you with us to protect Chloe. That tells me you can hold your own."

"His slayers were out of the territory. But yes. I'm not terrible at self-defense."

"Good. Train with me, then."

"Aren't you racing with everyone?"

Jack shook his head. "Tris can manage them for a night."

Dammit. So much for her bath.

ॐ

By TRAINING, JACK MEANT THAT HE WOULD relentlessly launch himself at her and knock her down, hard.

Fuck, the guy was strong.

But strength wouldn't be enough.

She spat blood on the floor and straightened her spine, climbing to her feet.

"All right. You can obviously kick my ass." There was no denying that. "But Seth will wipe the floor with your face."

"Do you have a brother complex or something?" Jack asked.

She had a feeling the man had something against her.

"I'm just saying it like it is. You're not fast enough, and I've seen no magic from you."

"I don't use magic."

Cat kept talking to buy herself some time, all the while gathering her strength. "Well, then, you'd better try to work out how to deal with this."

She extended her hands, and a lightning bolt flashed through the sky, hitting him right on his boots.

She grinned, happy with her aim, although she'd technically intended to hit the ground.

Jack glared at her, eyes narrowed.

"This was weak. And slow. Seth will be a lot faster, aim it properly, and fry your brain. Any mortal would die on impact. Some vampires could potentially survive. You? The first one might not kill you. But he'll summon ten more before you can recover."

Jack looked pissed, but he nodded. "All right. I can be faster."

"Faster is a start."

Promises

29

S he just had time for a quick shower before running to the pub.

"Cat! What will it be?" Chloe greeted her.

"Wine. Wet and white or red." She tilted her head toward Jack, who was sitting around a large table with his cousin, a beautiful brown-skinned witch Cat didn't know well, Gwen, and two other huntsmen. "On him."

After knocking her about for an hour, he totally owed her a drink. Jack nodded.

Cat had only entered the pub a couple of times, but it had always been packed. That Friday was no exception. She was surprised to spot Fin Varra in one corner, seated with Alexius and drinking something that smelled like well-aged spiced rum. He wasn't one to show his face much outside of class.

"Hey."

Bash. She recognized his scent as soon as the door opened. The man circled her shoulders with his arms, pulling her close, and the entire pub came to a complete standstill. Not so much as a fly moved anywhere.

Chloe cleared her throat. "All right, then. Nothing to see. Back to your brew, everyone."

The crowd attempted to resume their conversations, but Cat felt eyes on her as she advanced.

"Did you need to do that?" she whispered to Bash, who shrugged, entirely unabashed.

"I mean, I didn't need to, but I wanted to hug you. And I give nice hugs."

He did.

"Whatever," she replied, giving up. What was done was done, and short of erasing the memory, or killing everyone in the room, there was no undoing it.

Thankfully, the waitress, one of the Campbell daughters, soon arrived with a large glass of red.

"Anything for you, Bash?" the girl asked, batting her eyelashes like she couldn't see his arm around Cat's waist.

Cat did consider gouging her eyes out, but she quickly reined in her vampire instincts.

"A lager on tap, please, Mel."

He smiled at the waitress, and now Cat wanted to scratch his eyes instead.

What was wrong with her? She'd never been half that catty or possessive.

"Since when has this been going on?" Tris asked as soon as they reached the table.

Cat was quick to reply. "Nothing is going on."

Sebastian rolled his eyes. "Yesterday. Catherine is a goddamn ice queen about it, though. Somewhat predictably."

"Good luck, man," Jack said with a wince. "Better you than me."

Cat flipped him the finger before looking around the room.

"Searching for anyone specifically?"

"Yeah, Blair," Cat replied, without specifying why.

They occasionally spent time together; there was nothing conspicuous about wondering if one of her friends was around.

Sebastian did catch her eye, nodding knowingly.

"She tutors until eight-thirty, so she won't be long."

Cat killed time, nursing her wine and listening to the huntsmen's banter. As the minutes passed, she felt more and more nervous. She turned to the door every time it opened, although she would have identified Blair's scent before she walked in.

Finally, the bubbly, dark-haired witch arrived. She'd changed her hair color over the last couple of days, dyeing her bright red curls and black tips purple.

Cat rushed to her feet, waving her hand.

"Hey! Can we talk for a minute?"

Blair blinked, visibly confused.

They weren't really close. Blair was more Greer's friend, so their relationship was linked by proxy. Cat didn't even think she had her phone number, and they'd never spent time together without Greer. But Blair soon smiled and nodded.

"Absolutely." Cat doubted Blair was capable of refusing anyone.

She followed her out the door without asking why they were walking away from the pub.

Too many shifters and immortals with an acute

sense of hearing had a tendency to hinder private plans.

"So, I heard you specialized in charms, is that right?"

There were various facets of magic. Elemental was the most common practice, and the one most witches concentrated on, because charms, hexes, potions, and spells didn't affect the powerful creatures in the world. Besides, technology and science could replace all potions and charms, so why use up tons of energy to knock someone out or increase the speed of a horse when you could take sleeping pills or a car?

Some potion masters, such as Greer and Alexius, were strong enough to brew potions suitable for immortals. Otherwise, the craft was considered useless.

"Hardly. I specialize in people skills. And teaching. You know what they say: those who can't do teach."

Cat sincerely hoped she was underrating herself.

"Look, I need to ask for a favor. I thought about going to Greer first, but she has her plate full with her classes, Maddy, and everything else. Plus, she isn't into charms."

That Cat knew of. The previous day had proved she didn't know her friend as well as she'd thought.

"All right, spill. I'll let you know if I can do it."

"I'd like to contact my siblings."

Blair blinked. "There are phones for that, you know?"

"In a way that can't be tracked, intercepted, or spied on."

The witch laughed. "That's more like it. Who doesn't like a challenge?"

Cat looked up hopefully. "So, it's possible?"

"It's not impossible," Blair corrected. "Normally, we'd need a link, like an object spelled just for that purpose. But with siblings, that shouldn't be necessary. You are bound by blood. I can draw them to you during their sleep. That's the tricky part. You'd all need to be asleep at the same time. And there's a chance that they'd believe it was just a dream when they woke up."

That was better than nothing. "Okay, sounds good. What would you need? I'll pay you, of course."

Blair shrugged. "As long as I can write a report on it, I'll use it for a paper, so don't worry about payment. I'll need something else from you, though."

Cat winced internally. She preferred a clear exchange of funds to the prospect of owing anyone a favor. "What would that be?"

"Your word."

She turned to Blair.

"Just because the rest of us aren't allowed in secret councils on the hill doesn't mean that we don't get that something's happening. Something big. So, sure. I'll help you get in touch with your family, or whatever. I won't even ask why you can't just text them like the rest of us. But I want your word. Tell me you're not an enemy of our Institute. Because this place means everything to me."

Watching her closely, Cat realized something.

The huntsmen and a few vampires weren't alone against any upcoming threat. When the time came, the whole of Oldcrest would be by their side. If they trusted them.

The genius of Levi's plan was becoming clear.

"I give you my word."

"Good. I need to put a spell together. I'll send you a raven when I'm ready."

Mind Tricks

S eth was eating with his least favorite people in the world when he felt it. *Her.*

He was glad for the distraction.

He tugged on the pull at the edge of his mind, and felt the witch trying to bridge his consciousness startle. He grinned. She hadn't expected a response.

"Who are you?"

She said nothing, hoping he couldn't identify her. Trying to find an out. But she'd started this. He'd finish it.

"You will not return to your body again until I allow it, witch. Who are you? What fool would attempt to control the mind of a nephilim?"

"I'm not trying to control you, all right!"

The moment she spoke, he saw her clearly, as though she were standing right in front of him. The room where he was sitting disappeared, the food he ate became immaterial, irrelevant.

He kept moving, even talking, splitting his mind in

two so his actions wouldn't seem suspicious back in Stormhall.

But his attention was on her.

She wasn't what he'd expected. Only the strongest would have dared to enter his defenses, so he imagined an old, arrogant queen of some coven, at the head of a dozen witches. Instead, the intruder was just one girl. Woman. Something between a woman and a girl. She was in her twenties. Pretty. Her hair was ridiculous. To say nothing of her moss-green nails.

He believed her. She hadn't meant to control his mind. She seemed shocked to have managed to reach it at all. For that reason alone, he decided not to fry her brain until she screamed in agony and begged for a quick death.

Well, that and the fact that she was quite pretty. Despite the hair and nails. And the dreadful clothes. He'd always hated plain gear.

His eyes narrowed on the object in her hands. He recognized it.

"Ah. You're a friend of my sister, I see."

"She asked me to connect you, okay? I was just supposed to link your minds so she could speak to you directly."

That made sense.

"Tell Catharina I'll get in touch with her shortly. We have matters to discuss."

He should have let her go after that. He had nothing else to say to the witch. Instead, Seth retained her, keeping her tethered to his mind.

"What is your name?"

"Blair."

That didn't sound right.

"Blair the Witch?" he laughed.

"Like I haven't heard that one before."

"What's your true name, Blair?"

She narrowed her eyes. "Right. Because that's the sort of thing one tells creepy strangers who keep your damn consciousness hostage."

He grinned. She was frightened. Terrified, actually. But she had a backbone nonetheless.

"But you do have one. A name hidden beneath the mortal flesh. A celestial being inside you."

"Did anyone ever tell you that you're creepy?"

Seth laughed.

Only two women had ever dared. Claudia and Catharina. Blair made three.

Back in Rome, outside of the immaterial subconscious realm he'd entered, Drusilla's gaze focused on him.

He let go of the girl.

No matter. He would be in Oldcrest soon enough.

With most of the Stormhale warriors.

☙❧

"NEVER AGAIN!"

Cat blinked. She'd just stepped out of the dorm, and now there was a very pissed-off witch, index finger extended, glaring at her threateningly.

"Sorry?"

"I will *never* go anywhere near that weird sicko's mind," Blair clarified, stuffing Cat's diadem back into her hands.

Oh. Seth had...well, he'd been Seth.

Cat winced. "Oh God, what did he do?"

She shook her head. "I won't speak of it. I won't acknowledge it. It never happened."

Ouch. That bad. "Sorry. I didn't think he could affect you from a distance if you were just trying to connect us."

"Well, he can. Oh, and he gave me a message for you. He said he'd get in touch shortly. But that will *not* be through me."

On that note, Blair turned her heels and stormed toward the Institute.

Cat didn't think she'd ever seen the bubbly witch so angry. She shouldn't have been surprised; Seth had a gift for infuriating people like no one else could.

Cat made a mental note to ask her brother what he'd done to Blair. If they weren't on opposite sides of enemy lines the next time they met.

She headed to the printer to pick up the invitations; Mrs. Lowery had sent a raven to let her know they were ready. Then she headed back to the academy, following the narrow path to the birdhouse managed by the unpleasant witch in charge of in-house mail.

"What do you want?" Martie grumbled as she approached.

"I need to send messages."

The plump middle-aged man rolled his eyes. "No shit. How many, and to whom?"

Cat shrugged. "Everyone." Martie's eyes widened. She specified, "The teachers, the staff, the students, the employees in the town, and the shifters in the Wolvswoods, too." She opened her bag, but before reaching for the many invitations, Cat pulled out a money clip with a few twenty-pound notes. She removed the pin and handed him the notes.

Martie was a paid Institute employee, but people didn't generally ask him for so much. A little bribe wouldn't hurt.

Martie eyed the money suspiciously.

"That won't get the mail out any faster."

"Maybe not. And maybe my replies won't be accompanied by a curse or two."

He pocketed the cash.

"All right, then. Mail to everyone heading out."

Soon, the ravens flew back by the dozens. It was all anyone could talk about, and Cat was more popular than ever. People she'd never spoken to stopped her to thank her for the invite and promise to be there.

Cat had to admit: she hadn't expected so much enthusiasm. It was the end of term, with most people planning to leave on Saturday morning. That they'd rearranged their schedules to attend her little get-together was humbling.

A line had always been drawn between her—them —and the rest of the Institute. Vampires were other, darker, stranger, deadlier.

But it was fading away with little effort.

Levi had been right, it seemed. They could be allies, some day.

Although Cat noted that none of the wolves replied.

The Calm Before Him

CHAPTER

31

Bash drove one of Levi's fancy cars to Edinburgh. He'd booked them a lovely restaurant not even Catherine Stormhale found cause to complain about, and then they walked the ancient city aimlessly.

Old Town was lovely. Catherine wasn't one to be impressed by old buildings, that much was clear, but she indulged him when he asked if she wanted to see the castle. They stopped by a teahouse where she stocked up on supplies for her Sunday party, buying adorable little sets and posh teas that seemed far too expensive.

The point of today wasn't seeing a castle or eating nice food; he wanted to show her that she liked spending time with him. And that he liked her company enough to ignore everything and everyone else.

The tourists around them still smelled like food, but he and the dark, thirsty beast inside him didn't give a damn. He'd finally tuned in to the thing inside him. They agreed on one thing, and that was her.

"How did you like today?"

Catherine grinned at him.

"It was nice. Lovely, actually. Thanks for dragging me out."

He rolled his eyes. "Yeah, I remember a fair bit of dragging."

He suspected that her actually admitting there was something between them would take months. Years. Centuries.

He didn't mind. He had all the time in the world.

Bash pushed the breaks so hard the car swerved.

They'd arrived near the borders of Oldcrest.

And five lines of vampires stood between them and their home.

Most were old. He could have discerned that even before his change. Now, the age and power of the creatures in front of him was even more obvious.

Each of them was a force to be reckoned with.

And since they couldn't get through the doors, they hadn't been invited.

Shit.

"Drive."

He glanced at Catherine.

"They can stop the car. Hell, they can just stay in the way and let us crash into them."

"*Drive*," she repeated, more forcefully this time.

He shut his mouth, turned the key in the ignition, and drove forward, ignoring the hostile vampires whose eyes were on them.

As they approached the borders, the two hundred immortals converged on them.

He had to ask.

"Are you sure this is a good idea?"

"They can't get their hands on me. I can invite them in. Drive. *Faster*."

He nodded, moving his right hand away from the wheel to take hers and give it a gentle squeeze. She seemed lost, frightened, stressed. He had to reassure her however he could. For now, that would have to do.

She held on to him hard. Catherine wasn't one for sweet talk, or displays of affection, but her tight grasp was telling. She was holding on to him like he was a lifeline.

Her other hand reached forward. Bash could feel her call to her powers. A lightning bolt hit the ground, and some of the vamps moved out of the way.

Some.

Not nearly enough.

Bash winced, expecting an imminent impact, but just as they were about to reach the first row of enemies, the sky darkened, and clouds formed, shedding the sun of what had been a nice afternoon.

The next time, a lightning bolt didn't get in the way. A storm did. And hail. A precise, wrathful tornado forcing the vampires to move.

Bash lifted his foot from the accelerator.

"No! Keep going."

"Are you *insane*?"

He might love the girl, but there was an actual hurricane out there.

Shit. He loved the girl. He actually loved the crazy, beautiful ice queen. And he might die right alongside her. A little storm wouldn't have hurt two vampires, but this? Rocks the size of the convertible were being

219

lifted off the ground, dammit. Being crushed by one of those *would* kill them. The car was vibrating as if being shaken by a giant.

"Keep going," she repeated. "This won't hurt us."

She was certain. So certain he punched the accelerator hard and closed his eyes.

And then, the storm stopped. No more vibration. He opened his eyes.

They were in Oldcrest, in front of Levi, Chloe, Mikar, Luke, Ruby, Greer, Jack, Tris, Blair, Gwen, Bat, Chris, and everyone else. Some faces he didn't even recognize. All wearing gear. All ready to fight if—when —the enemy advanced.

"I can't believe you made it through!" Greer exclaimed, eyes wide with shock, as they got out of the poor car.

It was in serious need of a paint job now.

"We thought they'd intercept you. Damn, that was some storm, lady."

Cat shook her head.

"That wasn't me," she said.

Levi tilted his head.

"What then?"

She looked back to the border, searching the crowd with a frown.

"Seth," she mouthed. "My brother. But he isn't here."

Greer's head snapped north to Night Hill, eyes narrowed. "Someone just broke the wards." They all stiffened. "From the sky. It won't affect the borders elsewhere. The breach was right over the hill."

Catherine circled the car, heading to the driver's side.

"I have to go."

"Wait, I'll come with you," Bash said.

"You're needed here. Seth either wants to speak to me or is taking the hill for my family's benefit. Either way, anyone else stepping in would be fried chicken."

Dammit. He hated that she was right.

Bash's gaze followed the car as she drove back to the hill, half wondering why she wasn't just running.

But she'd used her power. Depleting her energy any more would be unwise.

When she reached the third house, he redirected his gaze to the enemies still waiting in front of the shield. For what? A signal? Seth?

"What are we dealing with?" he asked.

"The Stormhales. The Beauforts. All foot soldiers, not one member of either family." Levi grimaced. "This is the first wave. They're testing our defenses."

Two hundred seasoned vampire soldiers against the Institute.

Bash dropped to a crouch to rest while they waited. The shit would hit the fan, and soon. If his math was right, they might just win this round, but not without losses.

And if Levi was right, and it was just the start? They were screwed.

A Place

The wait was the worst part. The anticipation of knowing that, eventually, the line separating them from their enemies would fade. Fighting wasn't hard. Win or lose, it was a flow of movements—block, feint, lunge, kick, punch, and now, bite, he supposed. And at the end he'd either be the one left standing or he would have nothing left to worry about. A simple dance. But while waiting, his mind was complicating things, trying to predict the most challenging adversary. He knew he had to go for one of the biggest threats. As a huntsman, his duty would have been protecting the others—ancient vampires notwithstanding—but now that he'd turned, he had to keep the worst enemy busy, because unlike most of his friends, he could.

"I have an idea."

Bash was grateful for Chloe's interruption.

"Probably a terrible idea, of course. I'm sure just about everyone here has more experience in this sort of situation."

"Please," Levi invited her to speak, his jaw tight.

"You said they're testing us, right? Well, how about we deceive them? Then we can take them by surprise later."

Bash scanned the ancients' faces; most seemed surprised, some excited. Levi shook his head.

"You mean some of us could face them. That's a good idea, in theory. But it means potential loss. They may just be Beaufort and Stormhale foot soldiers, but they are rigorously trained." The ancient's jaw was set. "It's a gambit we can't afford."

"Everything we do means potential loss," Alexius challenged. "Your girl has a good mind for strategy. If half of us—"

"Not half of us," Chloe interrupted. "A handful of us."

She pointed to her own chest, along with Levi, Alexius, and the De Villier slayers. "If we go and ask to speak to them, make them believe we want to negotiate, they'll think they've already won. It'd play for time, if nothing else."

Bash was impressed. The semester was over, and most people should have left yesterday—and they might have, if not for the highly anticipated tea party on the hill.

Those cowards had attacked when the Institute was supposedly at its weakest. Making them think they were right, that Oldcrest was empty, was smart.

He chuckled. "I like it. Bet you anything they'll fall for it, too."

From what he knew of vampires, they certainly were arrogant enough to believe they had won by simply intimidating them.

"It's dangerous," Levi repeated.

"Everything is dangerous. Your girl is right, Leviathan."

The ancient glared at Alexius, who didn't so much as blink as he met the gaze head-on.

"Easy for you to say. You can't step out there."

"No. I'll just be the first to deal with the mess when they leave your carcass rotting on the other side."

"I can try to whisper to them. See if they'll listen."

"There's a difference between enchanting one mortal witch and a couple of hundred immortal warriors, Chloe," Greer replied, grinding her teeth. "But I think you're right. They've set up a trap, and doing anything logical, or expected, would just end up serving them. Some of us should stay here. Others should go. Make them underestimate our numbers."

Bash could tell Levi's silence equaled resignation. Finally, his orders came, curt and authoritative.

"Ruby, Luke, Bash, with me. Mikar, Alexius, you stay glued to Chloe. Do not let her step out of there."

"Wait a minute, I should—" Chloe's words died as the elder stepped toward his mate, each stride slow and almost threatening.

When he reached her, his face dropped to her, and his lips pressed against hers, briefly and ever so sweetly. Bash looked away, feeling like he was intruding on something far too intimate. Something he envied.

"You should remain *safe*," he stressed. "For me. I cannot do this while I worry about you."

Bash could tell she was pissed.

"I can take care of myself."

"You will. None of us will be idle tonight. But they

want you. Not me, not anyone else. They want to see you burn. This entire trap could be just for you. Let's see what we're dealing with first. Then you can save my ass when I need you."

The guy was smart; Bash could tell that spin would work even before Chloe nodded, her shoulders sagging in defeat.

He sent Mikar, then Alexius, meaningful looks. Bash pitied them both, if Chloe got so much as a scratch.

He glanced up at the hill, at the ominous single cloud hovering over it, before following Levi out of the borders.

Ruby was on the ancient's left, Luke covered his right flank, and Bash closed up the rear.

A natural place he'd fallen into without thinking things through. But it fit. Somehow, it fit.

Thunder

C at walked inside the ancient manor and found her sword still lying in the hallway. She'd left it there when she'd brought Maddy in, and hadn't used it yet.

She took it now. Lightning, Levi had said it was called. She knew it wouldn't be of any use to her now, but she still found it comforting. The sword was a present from Chloe, from Levi. A reminder of who she was here.

Just like Levi's house was decorated in dark red and silver, the Stormhale keep was purple and gold, gaudy tones Cat had never liked.

A handsome blond man lounged on a magenta damask four-seater, his head on the armrest, eyes on the ceiling. He wore a black suit without a shirt, and a red tie. This man was more handsome than Levi, Bash, and Jack. Only Fin Varra could hold a candle to his perfection, which didn't stop at his physical aspect. He was smarter than anyone Cat knew, stronger than most witches, and as good with a sword as any warrior, though he was only thirty-five. He'd turned five years ago, later than most born vampires. As a result, there was a masculinity, a certain ruggedness to his aesthetic. Messy hair and three-day-old stubble were his signature style, and he knew exactly how it affected the women—and men—he encountered.

No doubt he was the reason Cat was so hard to impress.

Cat didn't ask how he'd gotten in. She didn't ask what he was doing here. She did the only thing she could do.

Pulling her sword from its sheath on her belt and planting it on the floor, she got to her knees, head bowed low.

"Brother."

Seth rolled his eyes.

"Oh, please. None of that nonsense here. Aunt Dru isn't hiding behind the potted cactus, you know."

Cat hazarded a half-smile and rose to her feet. "That we know of."

"It's good to see you, Catharina."

"Likewise, Seth. What's with the dramatic entrance? I would have thought you'd quite like riding a bike through the Highlands."

Her brother laughed. "That certainly would have been more to my taste, but I'm here with a message that could not be delayed, given the situation."

"I'd say so. How long did it take you to get here from Rome?"

"Seven seconds, give or take. I didn't actually count."

She winced on his behalf. "Do you need some water, something to eat, blood?"

Riding a lightning bolt took so much energy that most storm mages would have died from the effort.

Most vampires, even those who couldn't use magic, could transport their consciousness to the mind of an animal they'd established a connection with. They called it syncing. When it was done well, they could literally disappear, their corporal form traveling along with the beast like a wave of pure energy. A form of blood magic born of affection and understanding between man and beast.

Some—the best—mages could sync with their elements. Cat had never managed it. But Seth Stormhale wasn't most mages. He'd mastered traveling through lightning as a teen.

"I'm fine," he replied, shrugging, like the almost impossible feat had been effortless.

Cat loved her brother, and knew that he loved her right back. But they'd never understood each other. He was a larger-than-life genius with too many gifts. Everyone in their family kissed his boots, even their aunt. They might be siblings, but they had little in common past their physical appearance.

"So, the message?" she asked. "A warning from Drusilla, I'd wager."

She wasn't one for small talk, especially with him, and with a few hundred slayers at their doors, now wasn't the time for it anyway.

Seth said, "Mine, Mother's, or Aunt Drusilla's? You have a few different notes today."

"Yours first," Cat replied offhandedly, though it might have been wiser to pick their aunt's message.

Drusilla was very strict about them calling her "aunt," though she wasn't.

Drusilla Stormhale was their great-great-great-great-great-grandmother, the head of the family. Everything she said had to take precedence.

"Mine is rather simple: don't."

Cat blinked in confusion. "Don't what?"

Seth sat up on the sofa. "Is that a new sword? Nice blade. Where did you get that?"

"Don't *what*," she repeated impatiently.

"Mother tells you to listen to our aunt, as she doesn't want you to get into trouble. Dear Aunt Drusilla says that all is forgiven, your treachery will be brushed under the rug, as long as you let our troops into Oldcrest right now. And I say, don't."

"I won't. I have a life here. Friends I value. Friends who value me. You can throw everything at me. You can torture me. I will not let our family destroy this place."

Seth rolled his eyes. "Didn't you just hear me clearly tell you not to do as you're told?"

Oh, yes. He'd mentioned that.

Cat cleared her throat. But Aunt Drusilla...

"If I don't, I'll be made an example of. You know that. They'll—"

"What, torture you again?"

She closed her mouth and looked down.

Mages of great power affected the very energy around them without meaning to do so, even when they didn't use magic. Their emotions, their movement were enough for the elements to vibrate all around them.

Cat had seen that with her aunt. Whenever she was angry, the room darkened, the air crackled.

She'd never seen Seth angry.

His expression didn't change at all, but his eyes were a dark galaxy with flickers of light. And the room grew colder, the air thinner. He took three steps toward her.

Cat had never been afraid of her brother until today.

"I realize I'm busy," he said quietly. "I realize I'm older, and that we have greatly different schedules." His voice held an edge. "And I also realize that I'm rather self-centered, but Catharina, learning what she did to you?"

Cat blinked.

Her brother had reached for her hands and was looking at the faint scars on her fingers.

"That was a long time ago."

"Yes. And the family doctor was so good as to inform me *now*."

His voice held as much thunder as his mind.

"You will stay here, where you're safe. And I will take care of our dear aunt."

That wasn't a question, it was an order, delivered with as much authority as any directive Drusilla had ever given.

"You can't. She's the head of the family." But it was more than that. "She is the first Stormhale, turned by Ariadne herself."

No other family was still led by their founding members. Most had died, the surviving ones had long turned into hermits, and, of course, there was Eirikr in his cage. But the Stormhales were under the thumb of a woman almost as powerful as the gods themselves.

"I came back from New York early yesterday to be told that Claudia was in the hospital. A broken ankle, they said. She was bruised too. Do you happen to know how she got those wounds?"

Cat looked away. "Our training was rough."

"They didn't train you. They brainwashed you into behaving, into believing that having a mind of your own would only lead to pain. Claudia told me what Uncle Antony did to her, under Drusilla's orders. She told me what they did to you." He glanced at her hands. "Have you ever played again?"

Cat wet her lips, finding nothing to say.

"This needs to end. They need to end. I killed Uncle Antony. He screamed and begged, but I killed him slowly nonetheless. I'm sure you'll hear of it soon. They'll tell you it was the work of some huntsmen, of course. And I will kill Drusilla, too. While she lives, I apparently can't count on your safety—or Claudia's."

He said all this very casually, without emotion or shame.

"You're insane."

Seth chuckled. "Everyone I know wants to use me. Everyone. The exceptions are my two sisters. Neither of you have ever asked anything of me. So whoever hurts you signs their own death warrant. Call it insanity if you will."

She most definitely was calling that insanity.

But she was glad Antony was dead. Glad he'd suffered, too.

"All right, what now?"

"Now, I bring you out by force. And we destroy your wards."

She stiffened, her eyes widening.

"What?"

Seth grinned, a cocky smirk she was only too familiar with.

"Do you trust me, sister?"

That was the question of the day, wasn't it? If she listened and he was spouting bullshit, all her friends would suffer. But if there a chance Seth could really be on her side, she had to take it.

Deceptions

CHAPTER
34

"Antoine. Gretchen," Levi greeted the two closest vampires to him almost pleasantly. "It's been quite some time. To what do we owe the pleasure?"

The woman he'd called Gretchen, a slender blonde who looked like she might chew metal bars for kicks, bared her teeth. Bash wasn't surprised to discover that they were all filed into pointed fangs.

"Since when have the Beaufort slayers needed a reason to visit their master's keep?"

"Since Oldcrest was attacked last winter. Haven't you heard?"

The woman growled. Antoine, a handsome bald man who had been turned in his forties or fifties, put his hand on her arm, appeasing her on contact.

They could be intimate. Maybe. Possibly. Bash would have banked on another theory: Antoine had a gift of sort, a mind control thing similar to Chloe's whispering.

Gretchen didn't look like she was intimate with anyone.

"Yes, we have heard," the man said, turning to Levi. "But we've heard more pressing concerns, like you've arrested Anika Beaufort without notifying or asking her family's permission. Our masters have reason to be concerned."

"I contacted Francois Beaufort according to our laws, and he made no reply expressing his concern. I believe he intends to attend the trial in London next week."

"Francois will have his niece *now*. She'll be in the custody of her family while we await the verdict of the trial, as is our way."

"Francois may have his niece if he comes to claim her himself. You know better than to think I would yield to a slayer."

Gretchen stepped forward.

Levi tilted his head toward her. "And what is the butcher of the Stormhales doing here? Any particular attachment to the Beaufort bitch?"

Bash couldn't help it: he grinned. Levi was seriously getting a rise out of them, but they weren't moving. Which meant they had orders.

"You've no honor," the woman spat. "Closing these gates isn't your right."

"No? I seem to recall, some hundred years ago, when the humans around here who believed they had a right to these lands put it up for sale. I recall writing and asking who was interested in financing this venture to ensure our history remained protected. And back then, the Beauforts, the Stormhales, and the Rosedeans believed that their funds would be better placed elsewhere, did they not?"

So that was why Levi was listed as the owner of Oldcrest. Bash had assumed it was some type of co-op deal with the rest of the royals, before.

"This is my home. I've allowed you to keep your houses, but this is *my* home," he repeated. "Your masters have no authority here. And their minions, even less so."

He was hitting a nerve, judging by the crowd's increasingly angry expressions.

"You will not let us pass."

"I won't."

"You will not let us recover Anika, a member of our household."

"I will not."

Antoine grinned. "You do realize this gives us leave to declare war on your house, Devil."

"I have written most of our laws, child. I know them better than you ever will. You may hold a siege. Good luck getting in without your key."

Lightning flashed above them, and the bald vampire grinned.

"No matter. We have another way in."

Bash's eyes widened, and he stepped forward. Right behind the line of slayers, a tall, handsome man with eyes he recognized had appeared, holding Catherine by the throat. He was ridiculous, dressed like a bloody knight, with a sword and all.

So much for trusting her brother.

Levi's arm barred the way as Bash tried to advance. He shook his head once.

"So that was your plan. Make the girl invite you in.

Not the worst idea," he admitted, his tone still light. "And then what? Who among you proposes to get past me?"

Bash looked down. His feet felt wet suddenly, and no wonder. He was standing in a puddle. And it was rising fast. One inch, then two, then five. He looked back past the borders and now understood why Levi had played for time.

The lake. All of the lake's water was traveling through Oldcrest, crawling toward them.

The slayers weren't unsettled at all, and Bash guessed that was for two reasons: first, Chloe's plan had worked, and they were underestimating their forces. But mostly because they hadn't shown their cards yet. The Beauforts and Stormhales had more in store, even more than the frightening mage holding on to Catherine.

"Many of us will die, that's true. But we are sworn to protect our house. When one of our masters is unjustly held captive, there can be no rest for us. Sir?" Antoine prompted, looking back at Seth.

The man smiled, his hand tightening over Catherine's throat.

"Come on, little sister. You know it's inevitable."

"No."

He lifted his hand to her face, a bright ball of silver-blue energy playing in his grasp.

"A thousand volts. While other Stormhales' magic may not do much to you, mine would be deliciously excruciating. I don't want to hurt you, but I will, sweetling."

Bash leaped forward. He reached Antoine and

punched the smug fuck right in the face before Luke and Ruby held him back.

The Beaufort slayer smiled.

"You'll be the first person I kill."

Bash didn't care about him. He didn't care about anyone or anything, other than getting to Catherine and punching the hell out of her disdainful brother.

"I will not let you through."

Seth sighed and pushed his left hand against her chest. She screamed, high-pitched and heart-wrenching.

And fake.

So fucking fake.

No one else got that. Not Levi, not the slayers. But right then, watching her artfully contorted face writhe in mock pain, Bash was certain. She was acting.

He kept thrashing against Luke and Ruby, not daring to give anything away. But he could have laughed.

Catherine was playing them all. Somehow.

Seth let go of Catherine, and she fell forward onto her knees.

"Is that all you got?" she asked.

"Yes, dear. Is that all you could do, really?"

The voice spoke seconds before she appeared, a woman similar to Catherine, although her hair was dark as night and her skin golden-brown and sun-kissed, like so many from the islands around the Mediterranean Sea.

Exquisite. And dangerous.

Along with her, in a smoky mist, twelve other elders appeared. A short man with the eyes and tongue of a snake, and a greenish complexion. A tall one, so frail he looked like a strong wind might knock him onto his ass, but his black eyes told another story. Each one of them possessed an aura just as gargantuan as Levi's.

No wonder the slayers hadn't been impressed.

Shit.

Did they have enough people to defend Oldcrest against all those ancients?

All the Monsters

"I suppose you always have been fond of the girl. Understandable, since you're bound by blood. Worthless and disloyal as Catharina may prove to be."

Catherine shivered, crawling backward. She couldn't help it. She always trembled when Drusilla was near.

"No matter. I can make her heel well enough."

Cat looked back to the borders. Levi stood up front with Bash, Luke, and Ruby. Bash was fighting to get to her, despite the hundreds of warriors separating them. Shit, the guy was sweet. And loyal. And hers. She'd done nothing to deserve him, but he was hers all the same.

Behind them, on the other side of the wall, everyone else stood so very close to the border, edging in. Both Mikar and Alexius were holding Chloe's hands, as if expecting her to rush forward at any second.

And, knowing her, she might.

They'd been smart to hide. Cat suspected it would have been a lot harder to draw Drusilla out if she didn't believe they were dreadfully outnumbered.

Still, too many guards were gathered around her for Seth to execute his plan. If he killed her, they'd be on him right away. Cat could see her brother had come to the same conclusion; his expression was cold.

Before them stood Credence Beaufort and Marina Slate, his long-term companion; Sylph Denningway, married into the Stormhale line; Fiona Hue, another ancient attached to Drusilla; and, more concerning, Julia Stormhale, Drusilla's only surviving child, a match for her mother in both power and cruelty. The others, Cat couldn't identify, but she knew that against all twelve of them, even her brother had little chance.

Seth had done nothing to her, holding a benign energy sphere that had only served to replenish her. But Drusilla was going to make it hurt. And if Seth attacked her now, he'd be doomed.

Unexpectedly, Cat felt a wet substance touch her feet, and she looked down to find water surrounding her, and also gathering at Drusilla's feet.

Levi. Levi was making sure that her aunt couldn't use her storm without hurting herself.

At least she wouldn't have to endure the oldest Stormhale's devastating magic. But Drusilla knew many ways to torture people.

Drusilla took a step toward Cat, grinning. She stilled. She should have gotten up, run, tried to flee. Maybe even fight. But that all seemed pointless.

She winced, expecting a blow she would have to endure. No matter what, the Oldcrest borders had to hold. They had to.

She closed her eyes as the long, sinuous fingers approached her, feeling a dark shadow drawing near, ready to tear her apart.

A sudden scream tore through the silence, ending as fast as it had come. And it hadn't come from her.

Something heavy fell on her. Heavy and wet.

Her eyelids flew open, her pupils dilated. Seth stood in front of her, holding her sword, Lightning, now thick with blue blood.

Drusilla's body was limp over Cat while her head rolled down the gentle slope.

She blinked, confused for half a second, then leaped to her feet and rushed to guard Seth's back.

"That wasn't very well thought-out, now was it," she commented as the slayers and ancients rushed toward them.

"Yeah, well, I panicked," Seth replied, handing her the sword. "You're gonna need this."

And she did.

Cat slashed the air just as the first Beaufort slayer reached her, catching his hand, then blocking an attack from the left flank. Sensing another oncoming threat, she pivoted on her heels and parried flashing claws. It was all protective mode; she didn't have time to lunge or feint or attack the constant onslaught of enemies. Fuck, they were strong. And fast.

A storm gathered overhead and fell down before circling her and Seth, separating them from the masses. She caught her breath, and had a moment to see that Ruby and Luke had let go of Bash.

Cat blinked, and a laugh escaped her lips.

He'd been right all along. He was a monster.

◈

When he watched the terrifying ancient approach Catherine, something unlocked in Bash. It had been there all along, beneath the surface, and for a time, he'd been afraid of it. Afraid of what he glimpsed when he saw his desires, his needs, his new instincts. But he embraced it. He welcomed the freak. To get to Cat right then, he voluntarily called the monster to him.

The ground underneath his feet shook, and without even thinking, he stomped his foot deep into the ground. The first line of enemies, the smirking Antoine and fangy Gretchen, along with a dozen of their pals, fell down as the earth shattered beneath them. He'd created a ravine, just like that.

Luke and Ruby were both wise enough to let go then. And he started running.

He only stopped to see Cat's brother swing the sword at his side, beheading the woman who'd threatened her.

Then he breathed and kept going, because nothing would be right until he was beside her.

Bash's steps punched the ground, making it tremble and crumble under all those who dared approach him, until they were smart enough to run. He reached the two vampires surrounded by a storm, and took one more step. Finally, she was there. Bash wrapped his arms around her shoulder.

"Never again, you hear? Next time, I fucking come with you."

She let him hold her until the guy behind her cleared his throat.

"That's my sister. This is way too much physical contact for my taste."

"Shut it, Seth," Catherine said. "And in case you haven't noticed, we still have a problem here."

Beyond the brother's storm, the ancients were zeroing in. Levi, Luke, and Ruby were being kept busy by the hundreds of others crawling out of Bash's pit.

"I can take one Beaufort," Cat said. "Maybe. Or keep him busy, at least."

"Point me to whoever I should bash. Let's see if I can live up to my name."

"Wonderful, a savage. You have excellent taste, sister. Try to keep the thin one busy. He packs a punch. I have to take out Julia before she destroys your borders. If she does, your little haven is doomed."

Bash didn't doubt that. The shields around Oldcrest were the only reason why the queen and her ferals, and whoever else wanted to get rid of Chloe, hadn't managed to complete their task yet.

Bash nodded, turning to Catherine one last time.

"Stay by my side."

She smirked. "Well, someone ought to watch your six, I suppose."

Spells and Shields

CHAPTER
36

Seth's storm cleared to allow them to pass, and Cat's heart beat at a thousand miles an hour, robbed of all safety. She'd learned how to fight. Her family had seen to that. But she'd always sparred. Facing someone actually intent on killing her was terrifying.

And she lunged all the same.

Before Oldcrest, she wouldn't have. She would have yielded, bent her head, fallen in line. Because she was no one. A shell of a person, built by others, stripped of wants, desires, feelings. Now she had all of that in spades. It was hers, and she'd rather be killed today than return to the shadows.

The Beauforts were well known for their skills as fighters, but their family wasn't blessed with magic. As an average fighter with a little magic, she would have been well matched against a normal Beaufort. The ancient was well beyond her skills, but she rushed at Credence anyway. The asshole smirked, knowing she was outmatched. She was going to have to make it hurt. For as long as she could.

Cat feinted, pretending to aim for the head, but dropped to the ground at the last second, attempting to trip him. And he moved in time, drawing his feet back to kick her in the face.

She ducked her head just fast enough to avoid the hit, grabbed at his foot, and pulled.

It wasn't enough. Even on one foot, his balance was perfect. Damn him. This time, she knew she wouldn't avoid the kick as he dropped his heel down to her face.

Shit, it hurt.

She'd known worse, though. Cat bounced back to her feet and yelled, swinging her sword.

Credence stopped the blade with his arm, then drew back his fist to hit her. It stopped right before meeting her face, hitting an intangible wall.

Feeling energy passing right in front of her, she turned in that direction to see Blair on the other side of Bash's ravine, both hands extended toward her, holding on to an immaterial thread.

The rest of Oldcrest had come out of the barriers. The huntsmen were rushing down the ravine as the vamps, mostly managed by Seth right now, tried to reach them to help with the ancients. But the witches remained in line, right before the borders.

Cat knew enough of magic to realize that holding a powerful creature like Credence was unbelievably taxing. She wouldn't last long.

And she wasn't going to miss that chance. She plunged her sword right into Credence's heart.

It wasn't a fatal wound—not to any vampire, and

certainly not to one as old as Credence—but he'd be out of commission for long enough.

Levi's waters had flooded the ravine, preventing any storm mage from using their magic—they would have just ended up electrocuting anyone. Thinking fast, Cat kicked Credence down the ravine and pushed one jolt of lightning right through him, before moving on to the next ancient.

Alone, she would have had no chance. But the witches—Blair, Greer, Gwen, or any of the others—slowed them down, hindering her adversaries' progress. More importantly, they shielded her so that she only faced one of them at a time.

They started to look like the winning side.

For a time.

Then the sky roared again. At first, Cat was unconcerned, believing that it had come from Seth, but the call felt different. More...refined. She looked up and gasped.

Her lightning, like Seth's, was a bolt of brilliant light. Nature called upon, unleashed. This was something else altogether. A dark bolt, zigzagging in black streaks, turning day to night.

Most turned to Oldcrest, but Cat's attention was on Julia.

Seth had tried to reach her, that much was clear, but the other ancients had barred his progress, keeping him away from their best weapon while she prepared to strike.

Now it was too late. She could see it. Julia had released all of her power.

Cat closed her eyes, feeling a shift in the energy around her, an explosion.

She didn't want to look back, but she couldn't resist.

The shields around their home were flickering away in crumbling bright speckles.

Anyone could get in now. The inhabitants of Adairford. The wolves in the wood. The younger students still in the Institute. They were all in danger now.

The enemies immediately tried to spread out, attempting to circle round their line of defense.

Shit.

"Seth!"

Julia was irrelevant now. They needed to stop the slayers from destroying everything in their territory.

Her brother nodded and rode his lightning bolt, appearing on the other side of the ravine, taking those who attempted to breach the eastern front.

But he wasn't enough.

Cat wished she could rush to help, but there were five ancients left, and only she and Bash were here to fight them. Even with the witches' help, they were outmatched.

Block, feint, run, roll, leap, kick, miss. Again and again. Stay alive. That was all that mattered now. Taking the next breath. Cat was tired, though, her limbs becoming heavier with every second. Bash was also slowing down.

From the corner of her eye, she saw wings. White wings. Cat glanced back long enough to see their second nephilim taking the other flank. Between Jack and Seth, the enemies soon stopped attempting to pass through their side, focusing instead on the center. On their witches.

Shit. This didn't look good at all.

"Pretty girl!" Bash yelled over the chaos.

"What?"

"I think I might just love you. You know."

What the hell? She glanced at him, a mistake that earned her a kick in the shin.

Cat moved away from Denningway to avoid another hit, and held her fists up in a defensive stance. The witches were getting tired, too, but someone gave her a window. As her muscles burned, Cat called to her storm, hitting the bitch with a zap right on her head. A little hit, but it was enough to give her a moment to slit her throat.

Then she turned to Bash. "Now? Now you go all mushy?"

He was on the ground, wrestling one of the ancients she didn't recognize. The man's fangs were bared, and he was closing in on Bash's throat. As she was too far away to jump in, she threw her sword, thankfully hitting the right target. Not fatally, but Bash managed to get to his feet.

Only now, the elder had a sword.

Shit.

"It doesn't look like I'll get another chance," Bash replied, eyes on his opponent.

Cat had another ancient on her right then.

With every passing moment, their luck decreased and the likelihood of them both making it out alive dwindled. The people who could truly rival any of those ancients were concentrating on Chloe. Cat got it. Chloe was everything to Levi, and everyone else deferred to him.

But with their ancients elsewhere, and their

witches weakening, she and Sebastian might actually die.

The vampires were getting close to them now. Greer had erected shields around them, but strong as she was, how long would they last?

So she said it. What did it matter, anyway?

"Yeah. I guess I might love you, too."

Nightmares

CHAPTER
37

The world was ending. He knew it when he heard those words from her lips. But he didn't even care.

Bash grinned as he faced his opponent, a man as wide as him, as wild as him, but twice as strong. He didn't think he'd ever been that exhausted. It didn't matter.

"Do you have any reason for fighting?" Bash asked the stranger.

"Honor," the man replied.

Simple and to the point.

And it sounded empty as fuck.

"Well, good. I'll probably win, then."

The man lunged, fast, but he wasn't the problem; Bash felt and saw another vampire coming from his flank.

He didn't have to wonder why. The witches who'd helped them however they could, ensured that they were fighting only one enemy at a time, weren't able to assist them anymore.

Shit. Two ancient vampires fighting him at once.

At least he'd heard Catherine say those precious words before the end.

He closed his eyes.

And opened them again.

The entire battlefield had been mayhem, brouhaha, disarray. Now there was complete and utter silence.

All eyes converged on the northern borders, so Bash looked too, frowning and not quite understanding what he saw.

The witches were still there, none hurt, thank god. Someone was standing in front of them. Some*thing*. Wilder than anything Bash had ever seen, stronger than anyone here. Something out of nightmares, protecting the nineteen witches.

He had no weapon in hand, no claws, his fangs weren't even out, but Bash knew this was a bloodsucker. No one had ever fit the image of a vampire more than this man.

He was tall and handsome. Too handsome. He wore a long, manly skirt—a little like a kilt, but black and flowing around his ankles. Nothing on his crafted torso. His skin was pale. His hair was dark at the roots, light after one inch. Matted.

Wildness and control. Beauty and savagery.

It hit him, then.

This *was* the creature of nightmares. Not Bash's, but *theirs*. All the intruders were living their worst fear.

This was Eirikr.

The stillness didn't last. The next instant, Eirikr's

fist ran right through the first enemy's chest, and he pulled out his heart.

A cannon. He was a cannon, bashing through the entire field with the might of a force of nature, the strength of a god, and yes, beauty too. His grace made murder a dance. Bash could only watch wordless, motionless.

The corpses that hadn't yet fallen to the ground dropped, and then there was more silence.

"Shit."

The abundance of blood all around him was making Bash sick, dizzy, and too thirsty. He brought his hand to his face and pinched his nose.

"Now, now," said Eirikr pleasantly. "I've known many warrior souls. I recognize greatness. That's just a little blood. You can take it, child."

Those words were all it took. Bash found that he *could* take it. That the blood was irrelevant. He straightened his spine and knotted his hands behind his back, watching Eirikr as he crossed the ravine.

Not walking down and then back up like everyone else. Oh, no. Eirikr walked on air, until he was standing right in front of the witches again.

They formed a united front, no one stepping away, no one moving. Bash had to admire them. Hand in hand with Cat, Bash closed in on them, and as he got closer, Eirikr's glare chilled him to the bones. If that thing had looked at him like that, he might have pissed himself.

Eirikr laughed.

"Who?" he asked.

Just one word, but Bash felt a potent authority drip

from it. He knew he would have answered—if only to say that he didn't know, or ask for details.

The witches remained silent and immobile, keeping their circle tight. Bash's admiration for them grew tenfold. After watching him dismember and destroy an entire army like they were nothing, they dared defy him? That took some balls.

Eirikr paced in front of the group.

"Eirikr," Chloe called, breathless. "How did you—"

"Escape? I didn't; I was released. By one of your friends here."

Every word had a threatening edge.

"One of your friends who has the blood of the elders, the blood of Tatiana, running right inside her veins. Who?" he demanded again.

His hand reached out to cup Blair's face. She tried to slap it away, but he'd already let go.

"No. You're a White descendant. Powerful blood-line. Not the *right* bloodline, however. I am looking for a dash of fae. A little Greek. A little Roman. Some Pompeiian...and whatever else you may have acquired over the last few centuries."

Now he stopped and turned slowly, grinning.

At Greer.

He looked her up and down.

"You."

She said nothing, but her chin lifted an inch.

"My, what an exotic cocktail. I'd say you're quite as beautiful as Tatiana herself. Perhaps even more so. I see some Indian, perhaps?"

"Yes, some," she replied.

"Among other things. It matters not. No blood could have overcome the legacy of your elders. And so, you're the guardian of this hellhole. The very last, if I'm not mistaken. I wonder what would happen if I rip open your pretty throat."

"Would you kill an innocent mortal, Primerius?" Greer challenged.

Jeez, the woman had a backbone of iron.

"I suppose I could make an exception."

She didn't falter.

He didn't move to strike.

"I am still tethered," he stated.

"I won't undo the work of my forefathers. I couldn't if I wanted to."

Eirikr tilted his head. "And yet here I am."

Greer lifted her hand. Though he was standing a few feet away, Bash saw and smelled blood dripping from the gash on her arm. Someone had bitten her. Hurt her.

Eirikr laughed. "Ah. I swore to protect Aurora. And so you used my words to bind me to your welfare. Naughty little witch."

He took one step forward, and Greer launched into a chant, words in a tongue Bash didn't recognize spilling out of her mouth at high speed.

The next moment, Eirikr disappeared in a blur, a fast shadow heading right back to his cave on the hill.

The silence returned. A silence charged with relief, worry, and questions. Above all, questions.

Greer sighed before walking back to the line where their shield had been in place. Her hands went up to either side of her face, and her chanting resumed. In the same language, but slower now, more eloquent.

Blair joined her.

"Do you want to channel me? I have a little energy left."

Greer seemed surprised. She nodded. "Thanks. That'd be nice. I'm beat."

She took her left hand and lifted her other one to match Greer's stance, repeating her words and letting Greer take her strength.

Bash had taken enough classes in magic to realize that, witch or not, he could probably help too. He stepped forward, offering one hand to Greer. Cat took his, then Chloe took Cat's, and Levi took Chloe's. Before they knew it, they were all standing in a large demi-moon, offering whatever energy they had left. Even Jack and even Cat's annoying brother.

And just like that, the shields were back in place, stronger than ever.

They walked back in silence through the main street of Oldcrest. Some went to the dorm. Bash followed Cat to Night Hill.

They reached the Stormhale home, and she led them to a bedroom. The bed wasn't even made, but they both crashed on top of it, fading into oblivion.

Peace

Sebastian was beautiful. She hadn't let herself admit how much until now, but he was. His eyelashes were so very long, his face so symmetric. And his mouth. She loved his mouth.

She grinned for the longest time, feeling incredibly giddy, girly, and silly.

She could afford to. She was alive.

Cat knew just what would make her feel alive right then. She got to her hands and knees and crawled down to his boxers, freeing his morning wood and putting it in her mouth, sucking it long and hard.

Bash thrust in slow and shallow, still asleep, but soon his eyes flew open. He laughed.

"I died, didn't I? I'm in heaven."

"We're alive, I think. But heaven can always be arranged."

She was too impatient to stretch out the play, too needy and desperate to feel him. She climbed on his lap and lowered herself onto his hard cock, moaning as he entered her. Thankfully, Bash was on the same page, and began thrusting high, hard, deep, and fast. Today wasn't about slow caresses, about sweet nonsense. It was about reconnecting, putting the pieces back together after they'd almost fallen apart.

They could have lost everything. For a time, they'd both believed they might. Now, they were reclaiming it. Seizing balance, perfection, life.

A bond. A bond Cat hadn't felt, but now tugged at her, making itself known, and there was only one thing left to do. Her fangs extended painfully under her lips, and she bit down on his shoulder, swallowing the tiniest drop of blood just as he took hers right under the collarbone.

One drop was all it took for mates to claim each other. And they were one.

☙❧

IT WAS LUCKY THAT SHE'D STOCKED UP. EVERYONE made it for tea at four o'clock. And everyone promised that they'd be there the next time Catherine held a party, and the time after that too.

☙❧

CAT AND GREER HELPED CHLOE MOVE HER belongings to Skyhall.

The dark castle was filled with light inside, thanks to its great windows. And something else. This felt a little less like a statement, and more like a home. A place where some might have laughed and loved long ago.

"I guess it's not so bad," Chloe admitted. "Wanna help me pick a room?"

She didn't linger in her new home.

She had somewhere else to be.

Chloe hesitated.

Even the very first time she'd made her way down to the cave, she'd been more confident. Even the very first night, she'd believed that this place meant safety to her. Now, she feared everything had changed.

But she went to Eirikr's prison nonetheless.

He was her ancestor. Her family. He called her his little daughter.

Yes, he was a thousand times more savage than anyone she knew, and yes, he'd done terrible things in his time. But that didn't have to change their relationship.

Did it?

Eirikr was seated on the floor at the end of his cave, his bright blue eyes locked on hers.

Chloe bit her lip.

"I didn't know," she said.

It made no difference, but she wanted him to realize that.

"I didn't know Greer was the descendant of the person who trapped you in this place. I had no idea she could get you out. I'll ask her. I'll ask if she'd consider freeing you, for good."

"Don't waste your breath." Eirikr's voice was darker, slower. "It will not be of use. Your witch's hands are as bound as anything can be."

Chloe wasn't sure she understood.

"Has anyone told you my story, little daughter? I

wonder whether there are any alive to remember it. Other than that monster."

He meant Ariadne, she guessed, given the ire and disgust in his tone.

"Levi might know it."

Eirikr snorted. "Your mate is a child."

Chloe chuckled, though there was little humor in it. She could count on Eirikr to say things like that.

"I'll definitely repeat that. See what he says."

Eirikr had no smile for her today.

"Tell me," she invited him.

He rose and strode to her. Lifting one hand, he placed it on the side of her head.

"No. Telling doesn't work. Let me show you."

And he did just that.

She saw the hills, smelled the freshly cut grass, heard the laughs and the chants. The scene ran at such a fast pace her vampire mind could only just grasp it. The beautiful woman he loved, the way he would have given everything for her. Then, his descent into hell after he did just that, giving his life so that Tatiana had a second to escape Ariadne's massacre.

She saw him rise again, and then walk away in the rain. Going to the only place he could go.

Tatiana.

She called him a monster, rejected him, threw him out in the street. Then there had been despair, for a time. Eirikr filled his life with the hunt, an endless game of predator and prey.

Hunting for Ariadne first, but finding her was impossible. She was too fast, too smart, too powerful. Soon, he started to notice the trail of bodies following vampirekind, and his prey changed. He hunted others like him.

After hundreds of years, Eirikr was as close to peace as he ever could be, settled in a beautiful land with three hills. Here. This was his home.

He invited the other vampires to join, building them a vacation home. As long as they were no threat to the innocent, he had no quarrel with them. He warred against the monsters.

He trained humans, asking witches to help strengthen them without turning them into abominations.

The huntsmen.

The witches...they were Tatiana's old clan. After the rise of Christianity, when they were chased away, he'd taken them in and settled them in a small fortress, right here.

The Institute. Clan...Vespian. That was their name.

And then there was a child of twelve, running away as fast as her little legs could carry her.

She had been conceived for one purpose: to be sacrificed in order to extend her mother's life.

Then Eirikr learned that Tatiana still lived. That through black magic and terrible spells, she'd managed to survive this long.

"I will protect you, child," he swore.

At first it had been just that. His need to protect anyone who deserved it, anyone innocent and vulnerable.

But then she grew into a beautiful woman, and it became more.

Much more.

He still didn't understand why she'd betrayed him. Why Aurora had locked him down here. That it was the machination of his enemies, he didn't doubt.

But the pain had not faded after all these years, and it would never go away.

Eirikr released Chloe's face now that she'd seen what he couldn't put into words.

He wasn't angry at her. He was distraught.

Seeing Greer had opened a wound he never touched if he could help it. A wound deep in his soul.

Chloe choked on a tear.

She'd once believed the world. She'd once thought that Eirikr could be a monster, or at least act like one.

No more.

"I will get you out of here," she swore.

"You can't."

Chloe swallowed.

"Why?"

Eirikr sighed.

"You'd have to kill the witch. And I will not let you."

Epilogue

EPILOGUE

Seth felt rather awkward as he entered the De Villier household. The great house was meant to impress, and usually, when he entered a home such as this, it belonged to him.

"Anyone here?"

The first thing to answer his call was a cat. A dreadfully adorable creature with a mischievous soul. He could tell.

"I won't fall for it. Go bother someone else."

The cat, somewhat predictably, rushed to rub over his leg.

"She doesn't usually take to strangers, you know."

Levi was standing at the top of his staircase.

"May I be of assistance?"

Seth grimaced. "I'm mostly here because my sister is getting fucked and I don't need to hear that."

Levi tilted his head. "An understandable position, I suppose. Would you care for some tea?"

"Please. Also, it's my understanding that you may

have a question or two about a queen, if I'm not mistaken?"

He had Levi's attention then.

"Indeed. Many."

"I thought so. I asked Alexius to run me through the situation here last night. I happen to know a little about that queen. And her island."

The vampire was at the bottom of the stairs within an instant.

"How?"

Seth shrugged. "I was there last summer. And if you want me to tell you, I demand tea as a bribe, if you please. Earl Grey, preferably."

"WELL?" THE QUEEN ASKED HER SPY.

The creature stood still, pupils dilated like a soul-less puppet.

"As you expected, the Stormhales did manage to break the shields, Your Highness. But they were rebuilt."

The queen's fists tightened on her scepter.

"How?" she demanded.

The spy's eyes clouded, becoming dazed and unfocused.

"I don't know. I can't remember."

The queen narrowed her eyes. A spell to confuse her spy. Which meant that someone in Oldcrest knew whose mind she was using.

She'd underestimated her opponents. For the last time.

"I suppose I have no use for you now, Easton. Slice

your wrists, please," she whispered softly. "Then I want you to portal back to the borders of Oldcrest. Be it a warning to your little friends."

"Yes, my queen."

The End.
Next in After Darkness Falls: Wickedly They Dance.

May Sage juggles multiple series and prioritizes those which are well reviewed. If you want to speed up the releases in the After Darkness Falls series, don't forget to leave a review!

More from May...

This was how she died. She knew it, felt it to her bones. There was no other way, not here. Saving herself would mean condemning every breathing soul in the city of night. As little as she liked most of them, and however much they hated her in return, she couldn't bring herself to destroy so many just to save herself.

She should give in now. Drop her bow, accept her fate. Yet she shot one arrow after the next, desperately holding on to life.

Devi took down enemy after enemy, her mind processing each kill with a cold, analytic indifference. They were relevant because she knew there had been fifty-one arrows in her quiver. Each fae she killed represented one arrow lost. There was every chance she'd run out of weapons before she reached the gates.

She was at the very center of the city, in the large Square of Dawn, famous for the obelisk erected at the end of the last war. The closest exit was a mile east, and there were three dozen enemies around her right now and more coming at every passing moment. It was a credit to her skill with a bow that none of them had managed to get close to her yet.

A horse whinnied to her left, and Devi's head turned sharply. She expected enemy knights. She'd managed until now because she'd only had to deal with foot soldiers; fae knights were another matter altogether.

When they came into the square from the south avenue, there were only two riders. She stiffened in alarm, until her eyes took in the colors of their habits and then their faces.

Devi had no issue recognizing the two males, although she'd never seen either dressed in anything other than their fine court attire. Now they wore plain reinforced gear under dark unseelie coats.

Neither of them looked any less intimidating for it.

"Vale."

The name fell from her lips in a tone she had never used to say it. With relief. Barely conscious of her decision, she adjusted her position to aim at the enemies following Vale and his second, rather than foolishly carrying on attempting to clear a path out of this nightmare. Vale was more important. If he lived through the night, there would be hope for the Isle.

Her shot hit the mark, killing a fae right behind the prince. As the enemy tumbled, Vale turned to see where the arrow had come from, his eyes landing on her.

He was on the other side of the square, but her vision could distinguish him quite clearly. For the first time since they'd met, he wasn't amused. His trademark smirk had disappeared. That shouldn't have come as a surprise given the circumstances, but his expression wasn't what Devi might have expected. Vale wasn't confused, shocked, or scared, unlike her. The dark prince seemed downright pissed right now. His violet eyes, so like his mother's, watched her with pure fury.

Devi's heart hit her stomach. Was this her fault? Had the attacks started because of her? It wasn't impossible at all, given her history.

Then, to her astonishment, Valerius Blackthorn, the dark prince, lord of the court of sin, lifted his hands, pulling on the reins to turn his horse away from the road leading to the eastern gate. Away from safety. Instead of heading out, he rode at full speed toward her. *Her.* The half-breed who was "nothing," according to him.

Devi regained her senses just as he reached her, in time to take his hand and hop behind him on his black mount.

"Fucking idiot!" he yelled before leaning forward and whispering sweet spells at the horse, who obeyed his master's urging, rushing through the streets of the city of night.

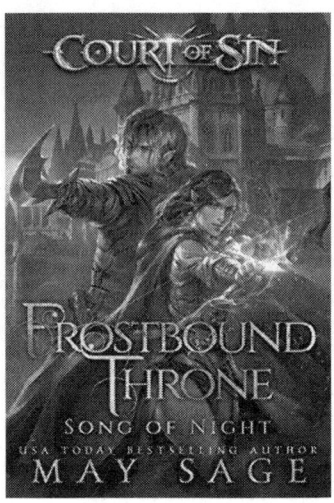

Available Now.

Made in the USA
Lexington, KY
03 November 2019